THE LIBRARY OF MUSICAL INSTRUMENTS

Kim Junghyuk

The Library of Musical Instruments

Stories

Translated by Kim So-young

Originally published in Korean as Aggideuleuidoseogwan by Munhakdongne in 2008.

First edition, 2016

Library of Congress Cataloging-in-Publication Data

Names: Kim, Junghyuk, 1971- author. | Kim, So-young, 1973- translator.
Title: The library of musical instruments / Kim Junghyuk ; Translated by Kim So-young.
Description: First Dalkey Archive edition. | Victoria, TX : Dalkey Archive Press, 2016.
Identifiers: LCCN 2016030333 | ISBN 9781628971514 (pbk. : alk. paper)
Subjects: LCSH: Kim, Junghyuk, 1971---Translations into English.
Classification: LCC PL994.415.C475 A2 2016 | DDC 895.73/5--dc23
LC record available at https://lccn.loc.gov/2016030333

Partially funded by a grant by the Illinois Arts Council, a state agency
Published in collaboration with the Literature Translation Institute of Korea

Dalkey Archive Press publications are, in part, made possible through the support of the University of Houston-Victoria and its programs in creative writing, publishing, and translation.

Dalkey Archive Press
Victoria, TX / McLean, IL / Dublin
www.dalkeyarchive.com

Cover design and composition by Mikhail Iliatov
Printed on permanent/durable acid-free paper

Table of Contents

Automatic Piano

If I hadn't watched a certain documentary film ten years ago, I may have become a great pianist by now. I was then a promising pianist under the illusion that my performance, even if given with my toes, could still make the audience cheer. I even wished sometimes that the piano had more than eighty-eight keys. My ten fingers were the only luggage I carried on my tours to different cities, where I performed music, pounding the keys frantically, almost convinced that the strings would catch fire.

I wasn't picky about the instrument itself either, unlike most pianists who'd stick to their favorite models. I was confident that my style could handle any piano. For instance, if I was to use a piano with dry and less reverberant sounds, I was confident to choose the right piece to match it. And for a piano with echoing and soft sounds, I was confident to give a performance to go with it. Although my confidence was not entirely groundless, I can see now, and I'm embarrassed to admit, that it was presumptuous arrogance.

Whenever on tour from city to city, I never forgot to carry with me a laptop computer equipped with a DVD player, so I could watch either the live concert DVDs of great pianists to get inspired with new concert ideas or watch music movies to absorb the lives of artists. Anytime, anywhere, I thought about the piano and nothing else.

While once reading Nietzsche, I came across a remarkable phrase. He wrote: "Without music, life is a mistake." I underlined it and added a note of my own: "Without the piano, my life is nothing but a mistake." Not that I fully understood what Nietzsche meant. I don't think I underlined that phrase because I understood it. I think I just needed an aphorism. As time goes by and I get older, I'm beginning to realize the gravity of what that phrase implied. And I wonder: can music fix a life full only of mistakes?

I was on tour again when I watched that documentary film. I was watching *Industrial*, a film by the renowned Italian director Salvatore Maranzano. I don't remember how I came to watch that film when it was neither a live concert nor a music movie. Nor do I recall what the film was about or who starred in it. The film featured the Mafia briefly, if I remember correctly, which I probably don't, considering there are hundreds of Mafia films out there. All I remember about the film was the piano melody used for its theme song. I loved it so much that I turned to the bonus features on the DVD, wondering who directed the music. On the second disc with a collection of bonus features, I found and watched the documentary film titled *Vito Genevese: His Life and the Piano*. That's where I first encountered Vito Genevese.

The scene of Vito Genevese's performance was an instant blow. It made my head spin, as if it were being beaten with a hammer. Whenever he touched the keys, my skin vibrated like the piano strings. I was almost convinced that the strings of his piano were connected to my veins. To this day, I still vividly remember his amazingly unsystematic fingering and the way his fingers almost caressed the keys. I can also see his hunched body sitting close to the piano as if to guard it. His body and fingers were the music itself. I could almost feel the music flowing out from where his fingers moved, even if the piano wasn't there.

The film, despite its title, was not about Vito Genevese's life and the piano. It was focused on the mystery surrounding the composer of many film scores who'd never shown his face to the media and never accepted any of the many recital offers that he'd received. Knowing that he was an aspiring pianist as a boy, one had to wonder why he refused to hold a recital.

Not surprisingly, the scene where he played the piano never showed his face, having pushed it out of the frame with a subtle trick of the camera angle. "Make sure that my face is hidden, understand?" he may have said while negotiating a contract before the shooting. Once he was done playing, he began to speak, with his face hidden, of course.

"Over the past twenty years, I've never been to the concert hall, ever, even though I've received countless invitations."

The moment he began to speak, I think I pulled my laptop computer toward me, eager to hear what in the world he'd have to say.

"Music is not created but dissipated. Music is everywhere, although we don't know where the sounds of music come from and where they go. At this very moment, music is also here somewhere. Therefore, the pianist isn't supposed to create sounds. His role is to use his body in dissipating existing sounds in the world. What I've just said may explain why I prefer distant and faint sounds. I don't go to the concert hall because it makes sounds feel too close and there are too many pianists who try to create music."

I couldn't agree then with what he said. More than anything, I couldn't approve his notion that "music is not created but dissipated." "What a weird theory of music from a mere film composer," I scoffed. "He may be great at playing the piano, but he still has more to learn about music," I concluded. Perhaps it was his concealed face that fueled, if not caused, my resentment against him. His disembodied voice sounded divine, not human.

He wasn't speaking with his moving mouth. He was transmitting the sounds produced by the vibration of his vocal cords. I hated the way it overwhelmed me.

I think I arrived at my destination before I could finish the film. I spent time playing the piano for audiences who might cheer at my performance even if given with my toes and completely forgot about Vito Genevese. After all, anyone finds another's story less interesting than one's own. I read newspaper articles on my recitals and attended dinners hosted by corporate sponsors. Everyone told me that they'd liked my performance and I'd reply that I'd liked it myself. I did think about Vito Genevese for a moment during an interview with a magazine when I was asked: "When you play the piano, what's on your mind?"

"Communication. When I'm on stage, there are moments when I feel that I'm communicating directly with the audience. That's when I feel really alive. Sometimes I get this feeling as though the audience were also playing the piano along with me. I call it true music."

In retrospect, I think my answer was more a criticism of Vito Genevese than an expression of my beliefs. And I was also hoping that Vito Genevese would read my interview, although the chances of him doing so wouldn't even be one in a million.

One year later, I came across the name Vito Genevese again when I was a model for the piano maker Partita. Since this company paid me quite a generous salary just to play the piano for a couple of shots, I was always trying to remain on good terms with them. In addition to salary, Partita offered me one of their specially designed pianos. They invited me to their headquarters in Italy so I could take my pick.

As soon as I arrived, I set out to find the piano with sounds that appealed to me most. This meant that I had to test dozens of piano models by playing each of them. The test was made tougher than it really was by the fact that I'd never had a favorite model, a point of reference, so to speak. On the third day I found one to my liking. It was a very sensitive yet blunt instrument. While it responded instantly to my touch to the keys, it produced sounds that were not soft but rock solid. I attribute my choice of that particular model partly to my fatigue. By the third day, I was beginning to see no point in choosing. Once I settled on a piano, the president of Partita, a stocky man with an unusually loud voice, cried as if he already knew exactly what I'd choose, "Good Lord, this piano is so popular!"

"What do you mean?"

"Oh, it's just that there's a man named Vito. And he picked out the same piano as you did."

At first, I didn't register the name Vito. I searched my memory, the names of pianists, for quite a while before recalling the name Vito Genevese.

"Is he a film score composer, by any chance?"

"Do you know Vito? I didn't think he was *that* famous."

Recalling the film I'd watched a year earlier, I talked about him, probably about how I'd found his piano performance amazing but thought his theory about the piano was kind of absurd.

"The piano featured in that film was presented by our company," said the president, "Not to brag, but Vito liked our products."

"What does he look like?"

"Why don't you see for yourself? He doesn't live far from here. He's a good friend of mine. He's a very wicked old man. You'll like him."

I had no intention at all of meeting him. I just wondered what he looked like. As I recalled the DVD that I watched a year earlier, only his body and fingers came back to me vividly. Obviously missing was his face, which had never been shown.

In my mind was a grotesque image, a headless monster playing the piano with its body and fingers only.

"You've come all the way here. Why don't you meet him?" suggested the president. "So I can see him, too, after a long time. Meeting him in person is the only chance to see his face, you know."

The next afternoon, I was packing up at the hotel, when I received a phone call from the president of Partita announcing a dinner appointment with Vito. I hesitated. Not only did I have a long flight the next day, I wasn't convinced that meeting Vito would be a good idea. How could I expect a pleasant conversation when I knew I wouldn't like what he'd have to say about music? Had it been an invitation to his recital, I would've accepted it without much hesitation. But I wasn't comfortable with the idea of meeting him in person. The president of Partita didn't understand my hesitation. After some internal debate, I decided to go. The reason was his performance after all. I'd never then and never since listened to any piano sounds that moved my heart as much as Vito's did. I decided that meeting a man capable of such a piano performance would be worth the trouble of sitting through an uncomfortable conversation.

We were to meet at the restaurant said to be the most famous in the region, not fancy but specializing in local cuisine. I arrived ten minutes ahead of time only to find that the president had beaten me to it. "This place normally requires a reservation at least two days in advance," the president said. "But not for a local celebrity like me." As the time of our appointment approached, I found myself fidgeting. That was unusual. I never fidget, even when I have less than a minute before my concert. I kept drinking the white wine that'd been served as an aperitif, half-listening to the constant bragging of the president. Half an hour passed, but Vito didn't show up. The president made a call with his cell phone.

"He's not answering the phone. I guess he's stuck in traffic or something. Shall we start eating first?"

We finished five different dishes in the next half hour but he still didn't show up. I don't remember what I ate or what we talked about. Instead, I remember what was going through my mind at that time. Feeling guilty for having started dinner without him, I was hoping that he'd never show up, and he never did. Two hours past the time of our appointment, the president also seemed to have given up.

"He's a strange man, I'm telling you. When I told him yesterday, he couldn't have been happier. Even clapped his hands. Do you know what he said? 'Oh, that famous guy wants to see me? What an honor! I'll have to get his autograph or something.' Maybe he's holed up in a bar, having completely forgotten about our appointment."

"Well, maybe some other time. By the way, what did you mean when you said Vito picked out the same piano as I did?"

He stared at me, as if thinking that it was a strange question.

"I meant you and he'd picked out the same model."

"Pianos of the same model don't necessarily produce the same sounds. You know how pianos are. Even the same artisan using the same techniques can't reproduce pianos with exactly the same sounds."

"Well, well," he said, laughing. "I can see that you haven't read our brochure carefully. I believe I've sent you a copy. The pianos that we make at Partita are fundamentally different from those made by others."

So began the president's unexpected speech. Drinking the grappa that was served as a digestif and eating the cheesecake, I listened to him quietly. "To make a piano," he explained, "you first dry the wood, and then set up the frame, and assemble the wood bushings and tuning pins, wrap the piano strings around the tuning pins, and adjust the pitches of the strings." The president went on explaining for a long time. "And," he continued, "after primary tuning the piano is sent to the soundproof room where it's tested with the automated machine pounding the keys hundreds of thousands of times." Finally, I was beginning to find his story a little bit interesting. "The whole process is concluded with modulation and fine-tuning, and this is where Partita's own secret recipe comes in," he said so loudly that the patrons around our table all turned to stare.

"We use a fine computer that enables us to express millions of tones. As you know, famous pianists have their favorite instruments. The computer enables us to make pianos that produce the same sounds as theirs."

"What about the piano I chose?"

"I have an album by an unknown pianist released about fifty years ago. When I came across it, I found its sounds very unique, and decided to use them in designing a piano model. The model was hardly sold. Customers usually prefer models based on the sounds of pianos used by famous pianists. They're fools. They believe what they hear is what they can play. Anyway, you're the second person, after Vito, to have chosen that model."

"But the tone isn't the only difference in pianos. The feeling of pressing the keys, and how the hammers work, these things also matter."

"Oh, please, come on. You should've read the brochure. It's all explained there. Through video analysis we can also express the texture of the keys or the intensity with which the keys are pressed. It's not perfect yet, of course. But don't forget that we are making progress. Someday Partita will become the best piano maker in the world."

Whatever he said after that was erased from my memory. Vito didn't show up after all, and I had too much to drink. I don't even remember what I was thinking on my way back to the hotel. Maybe I was reminding myself, "Don't forget to read the brochure carefully."

The next day, I boarded the plane, still drunk. Not surprisingly, I messed up my recital two days later. When I made a mistake for about the third time, the piano looked much wider than usual, the way the schoolyard had felt as vast as the ocean on my first day of elementary school. Thank God I could finish the recital before the audience started throwing stones at me. The day after I came home, my piano from Partita was delivered. The deliveryman handed me a large envelope along with the piano.

The envelope contained a note signed by the president that read, "Not to brag, but Partita's pianos deliver fast, too." It also contained two CDs and an automatic tuner. The CDs were, not surprisingly, film scores by Vito Genevese: *There Are No Roads in the Fog* and *Industrial.* As I'd already listened to *Industrial* before, I put *There Are No Roads in the Fog* into my CD player. The music was boring. Perhaps his intention was to create the feeling in the music that there were no roads in the fog; the tone and rhythm were loose, the composition too repetitive, and the piano not harmonious with the other instruments. I think I fell asleep in less than ten minutes, though I don't remember exactly. When the phone rang and woke me up, the music was still playing, leaving me confused as to how much time had passed. I felt as if I were really lost in the fog. I picked up the phone, without even turning down the volume. I said hello a few times but heard no response from the other end of the line. And then, with a cough, a voice blurted out of the phone. "Uh, this is Vito Genevese."

I couldn't say anything back to the voice that I'd just heard. I needed some time to make sure that I wasn't dreaming.

"You were listening to my music."

Only then did I manage to say, "Oh, Mr. Genevese." The song

from my stereo happened to be in a crescendo, reaching the climax.

"Over the phone, my music sounds not so bad," he said, and then paused, apparently listening. Meanwhile, I slowly returned from dream to reality, to my room, waving both my hands to dissipate the fog. I think the music took about five or ten minutes to finish playing but it felt to me like a very long time. And during that time, I wasn't listening to the music but looking at Vito listening over the phone. When the music was over, Vito resumed speaking.

"I apologize for the other day. I had an emergency, so I couldn't even make a phone call. Oh, how I wished to see you. Really."

He didn't sound untruthful. People with keen ears can tell from vibration in one's voice alone whether one is telling the truth or not. Similarly, they can tell if a piano performance is genuine or simply trying to impress the audience. Vito explained what had prevented him from coming to meet me, but I forgot about it the moment I heard it because I didn't think it mattered.

"Actually I wanted to see you, too, Mr. Genevese. I became a fan of yours while watching *Industrial*. I thought you were playing the piano like a harpsichord."

"Oh, I'm flattered. I don't think it was easy for you to recognize my music while watching the film. My music is usually buried in the film, you know."

"You've created really great sounds. A pianist should be able to recognize such sounds on first hearing them."

The moment I uttered "you've created really great sounds," I regretted it, realizing that I still felt unconscious resentment against him. But he didn't reply to my comment. I guess he simply took it as a compliment. Vito and I spent the next hour talking about film scores and my piano performance. For most of our conversation, Vito praised my piano performance. As it turned out, he had nearly all of my albums—the only ones missing from his collection were the limited editions released only in my home region. Although the president of Partita had called him a wicked old man, my first impression of him was far from it. He was a gentleman and a good listener, and he didn't forget to give me pointed advice where needed. In an hour, he and I had become friends.

"By the way, there is something I'd really like to know."

I finally asked him the question that'd been on the tip of my tongue. "Is it really true that you've never been to the concert hall in the last twenty years? Not even once?"

"I don't see why that should be such a big deal. Aren't there people who've never been there in their whole life? Countless people, I suppose."

"I think that's a completely different case. They don't appreciate music, but you are a composer and also a pianist."

"Well, I'm not sure what's so different about it. Anyway, I don't think I will ever be there again."

"What if I invited you to my recital, as a friend?"

"One cannot assure anyone of anything, but I probably wouldn't accept your invitation."

"I'm going to give a recital next month near the region where you live. I'll send you an official invitation. I'd like to see you."

"You're giving me a hard time. Just stay on your cell phone during your recital, so I can listen on mine. And have a drink with me afterwards."

I wonder what made me push him so hard. Perhaps I wanted to prove that he was wrong and I was right. The more I think about it, the more it strikes me as childish behavior. He smoothly changed the subject to the piano. After all, he and I were the only two people in the world who owned the Partita CD319 model. He asked me if I'd played it and I answered that I hadn't had the time yet.

"Then can I ask you to do it now? Do you mind?"

"I haven't even unpacked it properly yet. Besides, I'd need some time for practice with the new piano before I'm ready to perform for the piano master, wouldn't I?"

"I see," he said, laughing. "That was too much to ask, I suppose. Maybe some other time."

I gave Vito my cell phone number and he gave me his address. Before I hung up, I told him that I'd like to send him the albums of mine missing from his collection and that he could call me any time he wanted. I unpacked the piano and tuned it with the automatic tuner. The piano appeared to be in good condition for a product shipped over a long distance. I closed my eyes and pressed one of the keys of the piano. The key produced a nice sound, of course, but it also felt special to the touch—if I may put it that way. The keys are made of either acryl in most cases or ivory in some special cases. But the keys of that piano were made of neither; they were soft as silk but sturdy as an iron frame. I was completely captivated by the CD319 and played it for over two hours. I thought that it was the first time in a long time that I was enjoying playing the piano. "I'll have to use this one for my next recital," I even thought to myself.

My recital scheduled in the region where Vito lived was postponed indefinitely. There was some trouble between the corporate sponsor and the manager. I wasn't briefed on the situation in detail, but I guess it was over money. It was sad to lose the opportunity to see Vito, but I wasn't given much time to grieve, for there were so many cities that wanted my performance that I had to start preparing for another recital. By then, however, Vito and I were such close friends that we called each other every other day. Meanwhile, Vito listened to the CDs I sent him and sent me as many as five CDs of his film scores. The ones he didn't send me, saying, "You don't need these because they are copies of my old music anyway," I purchased from an online shopping site. I watched all the films featuring his music and found through a web search a couple of pictures of him, mostly taken in his younger years. None of them were formal pictures; they were just out-of-focus snapshots probably taken by someone close to him. No matter how hard I looked, the man in the pictures didn't come across as the Vito I knew.

"Would you say you are ready now?" he asked me during our phone conversation one day, meaning was I ready to play the piano for him.

"Well, I'm still uncomfortable with the idea of playing over the phone. I'd rather play in front of you. Why don't you come to my recital? I'll reserve the best seat for you."

"No, the best seat for me is right here. From time to time, I call friends of mine and let them listen to me play over the phone. That's a privilege that really close friends can enjoy. Can I have that privilege, too?"

"Well, yes, if you say so."

I played the piano. My performance that day wasn't excellent. Rather, I should say it was below average. Still, the recital over the phone was a really unusual experience. To begin with, I had no idea where to place the phone. If placed too close to the piano, it would interfere with the sounds. Too far, the sounds couldn't reach it. When I told Vito about my dilemma, he said, "Anywhere would be good. As long as I can hear the sounds, anywhere will do."

I pulled a small round table close to the piano and placed the phone on it. I wondered if he could hear okay. I hit the keys a few times, picked up the phone off the round table, and asked him, "Can you hear it?" "Yes, I can. Don't worry, just go ahead and play." I wondered what in the world he'd hear. I returned to the piano and started to play, but I couldn't really concentrate.

"This part should be heard, will this passage be delivered properly?" I worried as I pounded the keys. No wonder I couldn't play properly. As soon as I was done, I picked up the phone. He was applauding.

"Oh, it was awful. I'm so sorry. I couldn't concentrate."

"It's okay. It wasn't a bad performance."

He offered me words of consolation that failed to improve my mood. Maybe it wasn't a bad performance, as he said. But compared with my usual performances, it was terrible to the point of requiring a refund and an apology gift to the audience. I wanted to listen to him play the piano, but I couldn't that day because he had a visitor and had to go. For days after that, I was depressed, as if I'd messed up my recital. No, worse than that. I couldn't be in a good mood knowing that I had given such a stupid recital to a man who hadn't been to the concert hall for twenty years. An opportunity to hear Vito's performance came about one week later. I was fast asleep when he called me. No sooner had I picked up the phone than I heard him say in a hurried voice, "I'm about to begin playing. Are you ready to listen?"

I said yes in my sleep. I felt good, knowing that it was a privilege granted only to close friends of his. From afar, really afar, piano sounds began to come to my ears. "How large is his house?" I wondered. As I strained my ears to catch the barely audible sounds, I fully awoke from sleep before I knew it and found myself closely listening to him play with my ears glued to the phone. "Make the sounds faint as if from afar" seemed to be the instruction written all over his score. Soft and faint sounds came over to me through the phone. It was a sequence of punctuated sounds rather than music. Each of the piano sounds was manifesting itself as an independent object, not as a part of music. I thought of a scene in an animated film where a note appeared and floated up in the air whenever the pianist hit the keys.

The notes that gathered in the air made their way onto the score and soon turned into music. Listing to him play, I was reminded of that scene. When I closed my eyes, I thought I could see the notes.

When he finished playing after about half an hour, I sprang from my bed to applaud him with all my heart, clapping my hands with the phone placed between my neck and shoulder. Even though he couldn't see whether I was standing on my feet or lying on my back, I tried to show respect for him in my applause.

"What do you think? How did you like my first performance?"

"Bravo!"

"No encore, please," he insisted, laughing. "I'm not in such good condition today. I was kind of nervous playing before a famous pianist."

"Don't say that. You're not teasing me, are you?"

"Of course not, it's just that the piano is getting harder and harder for me. I guess I'm a little too old now to handle it."

"Listening to your piano sounds today, I'm all the more eager to see you in person. If I'm there, will you play the piano for me?"

"Well, I'm sure you'll find plenty of things that are more entertaining than that. I'd like to see you, too."

"I don't think there's anything that'll be more entertaining than your piano performance."

"When you're here, let's go to see the ocean together. She's a good player, too." He laughed.

I think that was when it started. Once I listened to Vito's phone performance, I began to think of the piano a little bit differently than before. I began to ask myself: "How do sounds that come together make music? Are sounds generated spontaneously or are they created? What makes sounds different from music?" I also began to ponder what he'd said on the DVD. But those questions were too profound for me to find answers for myself.

I once asked Vito, a few days before he died, why he liked my piano performance. He seemed startled by my question. He couldn't answer it readily. By then, his health had already deteriorated considerably. It was my complete ignorance of his condition, of course, that allowed me to ask him such a stupid question. He was panting—from which I should have noticed his looming death; after all, a man is less interested in another's story than in his own—as he said, "I think I like your performance because it feels transparent. It gives me the impression that you're faithfully reproducing each and every note on the score without trying to interpret or analyze anything. That's a good talent."

"I do analyze, though, from time to time."

"I know, I know. But still transparent. You know what? I believe that's what the artist should be. I believe that the artist is supposed to lend his whole body to art."

"I don't like the idea of lending."

"Well, you don't have to when you don't feel like it. When I hear you play the piano, I feel that it sounds like automatic piano."

I never had the chance to attend Vito's phone recital again. Moreover, I never had the chance to meet him, not even once. I could have if I hadn't been so lazy. But I feel that perhaps we weren't meant to meet each other. It was better for our relationship. When I found his obituary in a corner of the newspaper, I felt as if I were being hammered in my chest. When I talked to him over the phone a few days before his death, he was making a joke, even then.

When the president of Partita called me, I lost my temper, blaming him for not having told me that Vito had been in poor health. But I knew he wasn't really to blame. The president of Partita said that he hadn't met Vito for over three months. Living closer to Vito—even if through the phone line—was me.

The president gave me the funeral schedule over the phone, but I didn't go. Instead, I stayed home and remembered him alone, watching a few films for which he'd written scores and re-watching the documentary film included in *Industrial.*

I'm still not sure if automatic piano is something good or bad. Although I know he meant it well when he said it, all that term brings to mind is what could have been a scene from a horror film, where a haunted piano plays itself. I still don't understand what it means to lend one's whole body to art either, although I think I have an inkling now of why he'd never go to the concert hall.

After his death, a small memorial concert for him was held in the region where I lived. Arranged jointly by the film and music communities, the concert would feature an orchestra and the piano performing his hit film scores. I was obviously not invited to the concert because no one knew about my intimate friendship with him. I went and watched the concert in a seat for the general audience. The irony of the concert struck me. A concert remembering a composer who hadn't been to the concert hall since he was thirty.

I couldn't concentrate on the concert. Immensely popular and pleasing as they were, his songs failed to move me, even played by a good orchestra and a good pianist. Throughout the concert, I wondered why. On my way home afterwards, I missed his performance over the phone so much, a performance that was composed of soft and solid sounds that sounded like crickets and also like waves. I was exasperated by the hard truth that it was impossible to hear his performance anymore. Back home, I pounded the keys. While it was the same piano as his, with every feature made identical by the latest fine computer, I couldn't even begin to imitate his performance. I tried listening to my own performance over the phone through headphones connected to it. But what I heard wasn't music. It was nothing but noise generated when the pressed keys triggered the hammers to touch the strings.

A few days after his memorial concert, I went to another concert. A pianist who was a long-time acquaintance of mine had invited me to his recital. There, I understood what Vito had said. As in his memorial concert, I couldn't concentrate on music. I wasn't hearing it. I noticed the pianist's techniques and facial expressions instead of his music. The pianist was expressing music with all kinds of facial expressions and gestures. I was probably no different from him in my own recitals.

Music, after all, wasn't simply composed of sounds. Music in the concert hall was created as the piano sounds blended with the pianist's gestures, movements of his fingertips and feet, his facial expressions, and the sounds of the audience clearing their throat and clapping their hands. Vito was displeased with all those other elements interfering with music. As he said, all the sounds were too close and alive. The pianist looked as though he were inventing new music on the spot.

I'm still a pianist. I give a recital once in a while and release an album every few years, though not as often as before. But I'm not sure if I'm really a pianist. If I hadn't watched a certain documentary film ten years ago and so hadn't met Vito, would I have become a great pianist? Again, I'm not sure. If I'd continued to play like an automatic piano, as Vito had put it, would I have become a better pianist than I am now? Whenever I face such a question from within myself, I remember what Vito said: "Music isn't created but dissipated." It troubles me but also comforts me sometimes. I am comforted by thinking that with each piano key I press, certain music in the world penetrates through my body and then dissipates like smoke. Where does all the dissipated music go? Is it just gone? I hope that it all goes to Vito.

Manual Generation

I STILL HADN'T WRITTEN the first sentence yet. I was already stuck in Precautions. Writing Precautions for common items is a piece of cake. Just copy and paste the old ones, with some rewording and rearrangement. For instance, replace "it could be dangerous" with "it is dangerous" and "disassembling could cause a severe shock" with "do not disassemble." But this doesn't work for a product with features that I haven't seen before. In this case, no amount of explaining can get me unstuck, and I have to think hard to figure out which warning should come first. I believe in order and organization, even in the most useless manual.

I still remember the first manual I ever saw in my life: the manual of a digital camera purchased with pocket money I'd saved for months. When I opened the package that came in the mail, I was overwhelmed. Not by the product but by its 300-page manual. Without even thinking about unpacking, I started reading the manual for fear that I might break the camera if I started using it without reading the manual first. I spent all night reading and rereading carefully from cover to cover: Precautions, Parts & Components, Getting Ready to Take Pictures, Basic Features, Advanced Features, Tips on Taking Nice Pictures, Appendices, and Specifications. I was moved by it. The manual drew a large blueprint on the flat surface in my head and then built on it an elaborate structure of knowledge made of texts, figures, and tables. Completed in my head was a town owned by the digital camera. I found that architecture fascinating. Once I finished reading the manual, I thought I'd understood what the digital camera was.

Then I began collecting manuals. They gave me the illusion of having used the products without owning them. I downloaded free manuals in PDF format from the web and scrounged up free copies of all sorts of manuals from the salesclerks at the electronics stores.

My experience of reading hundreds of manuals so far tells me that there are two kinds of manuals in the world: good ones and bad ones. Good manuals draw a huge blueprint in my head, whereas bad ones leave me with a pile of random information as shaky as a sandcastle. Good manuals convince the user with logic, whereas bad ones are so self-centered that they're unkind to the user. I'm inclined to believe that people who make bad manuals must be bad people.

"You haven't even started yet," said Park, our design manager, looking at my monitor. Annoyed as I was by the mocking tone of his voice, I kept my temper, because he and I were on a team together that made good manuals and therefore he couldn't be a bad person.

"It's your fault. You signed this deal without my permission."

"Excuse me? You're the one who told me to go out and find deals. Okay, I'll cancel it then."

"No, you can't do that. I've got office rent to pay."

"Then finish your writing. You've got employees to pay, too. The product illustration is almost done, by the way."

"You sound like you're the boss. I think you'd have my hands tied to the keyboard if you were really the boss."

"Wrong. I would've already fired you. You're doing so little for what you get paid, and whining so much."

"Enough. I'll finish my writing by tomorrow. So stop bugging me and get lost."

Park returned to his desk, sipping his coffee. My eyes returned to the monitor, a bleak desert with nothing but the black cursor blinking. The blinking cursor came across as an SOS from someone buried in the desert. "Look, I'm just about as suffocated over here as you are over there. Consider staying buried, okay? Don't send off SOSs. There's no one out here to help you anyway." But I also felt like sending off an SOS to someone in the desert.

"I think I need to take a look at the product illustration file first. Send it over, will you?" I shouted at Park. My voice was so loud that it caused all three of my employees to look at me. Even though it wasn't unusual for me to be on edge trying to make a manual in time before product release, I think I was edgier than usual for this one. The employees looked uneasy, as though they were handling a ticking time bomb.

"It's not done yet. Why don't you play with the product first before you start?"

"I already did so many times that my hands went numb. No inspiration. Just send it over. I don't care if it's not done," I shouted in a voice loud enough to reach the back of an auditorium. But our office would actually be less than one-fifth its size. Our staff consists of four members, including myself, the boss. The rest include one manager and one intern, which leaves only one position for an ordinary employee. What an imbalanced organization! Adding to this imbalance is the fact that the four of us are all male. Park sent me a file, and I opened it to find:

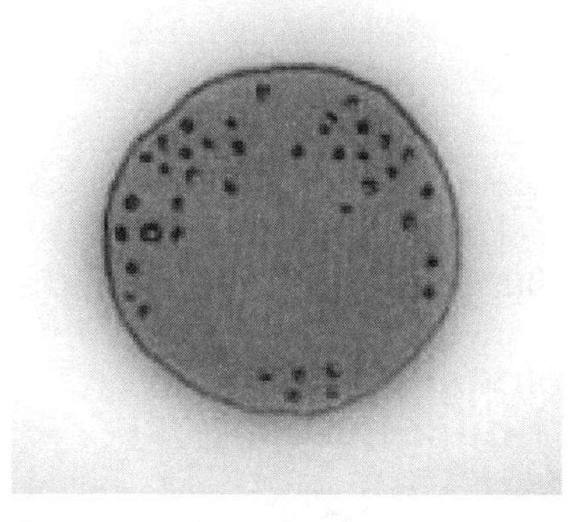

"What is this? Are we working on a manual for spherical cheese? Or a manual for a golf ball?"

Park walked over to my desk. He took a look at the monitor and laughed. "Wrong one. This is one of the initial sketches."

"You waste time. No wonder our company isn't making enough money to pay office rent. You send me the wrong file, walk over here, walk back to your desk, and send me another file, and I open it. If I added up all this time . . ."

"I know you're not good at math, boss. So I know you'd waste more time trying to add it all up."

"I'm the boss here. How come I'm not respected by my employee? What kind of company is this?"

"A fine company."

I saw the rest of the employees laughing, their faces turned away toward the window. I almost burst into laughter myself but managed to suppress it. Whenever I was on edge, Park would try to make me laugh. When he was on edge, it would be my turn to make him laugh. It was kind of a give-and-take deal.

Park sent me another file. Instead of opening it, I continued to examine his sketch. It was sitting at the center of the monitor and staring at me. It came across as a planet in the universe, an only-survivor named "Golf Ball" with all the other planets gone. It looked lonely. There was suspense in the sketch, an ominous feeling that a golf club would appear out of nowhere and smash the planet "Golf Ball" out of the universe. With its last planet gone, the universe would be left empty except for the solemn voice of God saying, "Nice shot!"

"What was the name of this product again, Park?"

"The Global Player."

"That's a lousy name."

"Tell it to the client's publicist when she gets here. She'll be here in half an hour."

"What? Who told you to make an appointment with her?"

"Don't worry. She's coming to see the illustration, not the text, although she wouldn't be so happy if she found out that you haven't even started writing yet. I guess you could buy some time if you told her that you think the product has a lousy name. I'd say it'd take them at least a month trying to rename the product. Another possibility is that she may decide to leave us for another company. That'd be fine by us, except that you'd still have the lousy office rent to pay."

"Be quiet, all of you. Can't you see I'm writing now?"

All of them had been quiet all along, being hard at work, except for Park and me. I put on my headphones and set to work. I felt ready to write anything, knowing that the deadline was only half an hour away. There was a stack of developer's handbooks to my left, the illustration file sent by Park open in the monitor, and the product to be released under the lousy name "Global Player" to my right. I was all set. I began to write the first sentence.

When using the Global Player, use the same precautions that might apply to the Earth. Regard the Global Player as the Earth.

First, don't disassemble. Second, don't store at high temperatures. Third, don't drop. Imagine that you're God, the creator of the Earth. Then you wouldn't want to throw the Earth around. Most importantly, keep the Earth out of the reach of children. Otherwise, they'd certainly destroy the Earth.

I completed one sentence after another, listening to a song that a native African tribe may have used while hunting. Once I finished the first sentence, the next ones began to present themselves bit by bit. In my experience writing manuals, it always seems as though hidden sentences make a reluctant appearance, as opposed to my writing them. It makes me wonder if the art of writing manuals is closer to excavation than to creation. My job is simply to beat the dust off the sentences. That makes me an archeologist.

I finished Precautions in twenty minutes. I read the first sentences to Park, who replied with "Not bad." According to Park's Conversational Dictionary, "not bad" means "good." Encouraged by his compliment, I rushed through Parts & Components and Basic Features. These aren't the parts that take very long to finish, as long as I refer to the developers' handbooks for paraphrase and translation.

When I started writing the Advanced Features section, the office door opened and a woman in a black two-piece suit entered. At that moment, I was listening to a sad ballad by a passionate Greek singer. On seeing the woman in black, I felt as though the music were turning our office into a funeral home. Her tall and stout body added to the solemn mood. I took off my headphones, whereupon her voice reached my ears. It was a shrill voice that didn't match her body. She was talking with Park without even looking at me. I pretended not to have noticed her, when Park introduced me. She handed me her business card.

"I heard a lot about you. I hear you're writing the manual of our product yourself. I appreciate it."

"My pleasure. It gets me listening to a lot of music, which I love. It's such an intriguing product that I'm having fun writing a manual for it."

"I look forward to reading it."

She gave me a nod before walking over to Park's desk. Looking at her up close, I found she wasn't a funeral type. Her face wasn't pretty but bright, so bright that a smile would make it shine and pierce any surrounding darkness.

I put my headphones back on and went back to work, but kept the volume down, eager to eavesdrop on the conversation between her and Park. There was nothing extraordinary about their conversation. I prefer this to that. Yes, I'd prefer if the illustration had a softer feeling. How about using more blue? No, I mean, I love it overall. I'd just prefer if it had a brighter tone. While writing, I stole brief glances at her. I found her smiling a lot. Whether it meant she was being polite or enchanted by Park, I wasn't sure. She gave a smile, baring her teeth, at least every thirty seconds. I couldn't excavate new sentences, not even a single one, until she left.

After two full days of effort, the manual was completed. Park and I have the ritual of rating our manuals once they're done. We gave the Global Player eight out of ten points. Eight points is an excellent mark. Most manuals receive seven, and a full mark of ten has been given only once. Many of our clients would be outraged if they found out about our rating ritual. "Six points? Are you kidding me? Improve it until it becomes perfect!" some of them would demand. But they don't understand. If we could improve it, we'd be more than happy to do so. I believe that all manuals have their own fate. A good manual is born when a creative product, fine illustrations, and well-written texts come together in perfect harmony. A mediocre product is destined to get a mediocre manual. Garbage in, garbage out.

After transmitting the completed manual to the client, we went to a wine bar near the office for a belated welcoming party for the intern who'd joined us a month earlier. The occasion had been delayed due to the recent rush of work.

"Intern, which one would you like?" I handed him the wine list. The intern stared at it. He leafed through it page by page before he handed it back to me. "I don't care. Why don't you order for me, boss?"

"We're here for you. You should take your pick."

"I don't know much about wine."

"What's there to know about it? Listen. The first thing you should learn about writing good manuals is classification. You should know which features to present together and which precautions to put together. Those are the ABCs. And you should be also able to tell good manuals from bad ones just by taking one look at them. Tell me what you think about the classification of the wines on this list."

"I think they're classified by country."

"And by something else, too. First, by country: France, Italy, Australia, etc. Second, by type: red wine, white wine, sparkling wine, etc. But don't limit yourself to these kinds of classifications. New classifications are also possible."

"Such as?" The intern listened intently, with both his hands placed neatly on his lap. Park butted in.

"His classification is simple. He sees that there are three types of wine: over 100,000 won, between 50,000 won and 100,000 won, and below 50,000 won. Which one are you going to choose? For your information, Intern, our boss is especially fond of wines below 50,000 won. He's got to save money on wine bills to pay his office rent."

"No, not today, Park. I'm telling you. You know we've finished the lousy Global Player. Once we receive the money, it'll take care of the rent right away. All right, a special treat today. Let's go for wines near the 100,000-won range."

I ended up spending 600,000 won for the night but didn't feel bad about it. I realized that it could be fun to be among a group of four men talking in a wine bar. Quick Mouse of the design team—the only ordinary employee at our company, who believes himself to be world champion in mouse-moving speed—was drunk and had fallen into the habit of hugging the intern; Park badmouthed me for half an hour while no one listened; and I dozed off quietly. As I became tipsy from the wine, I found myself more and more drowsy. But I felt happy in my sleepiness. I thought that the intern had finally completed our team by joining in. A team of four is definitely better than a team of three. Park, Quick Mouse, and the intern headed to a different place for more drinks and I went home and collapsed into bed.

When Park called me the next morning, I'd just woken from a sleep that deserved a full mark of ten, and was staggering on the rope hanging between sleep and reality.

"Have you woken up?"

"Not yet. I'm talking in my sleep. Once I wake up, I won't remember anything you said. So tell me now if it's bad news. If it's good news, call me again later."

"Goscinny called. She was looking for you."

"Goscinny? Do I know her?"

"She's the client for the lousy Global Player. She told me to tell you to call her."

"This can't be good."

I turned on my laptop and opened the Global Player manual file. I knew that the client would never look for me, the president, at least not for something minor like the omission of an important feature or a mistake in Parts & Components. It had to be something truly bad, like a critical mistake or the omission of an important section. I reviewed the manual but found nothing resembling a critical mistake. When I called Goscinny, she told me something I didn't expect to hear. "I've read through the manual this morning."

"You have? I didn't think it would make such a good morning read."

"I was moved by it."

"Excuse me? I'm not sure if I heard you correctly."

"I read it through in one hour and found it so touching."

"Are you sure you have the right file? It's a manual with Precautions and Parts & Components, not a poem or novel . . ."

"It was the manual of my dreams. Can you spare a few minutes this afternoon? I have something to tell you in person."

After hanging up the phone, I reviewed the manual again in a futile attempt to find any parts that may have moved her. She was the first person that I'd ever known, other than myself, who'd been moved by a manual she'd read. I know saying this would be an insult to myself, but I must say that the kind of people who read a manual and say that they were moved by it can't be normal. Being moved by something is a very personal emotion, certainly, but I believe that it should still make sense.

When I arrived at the coffee shop, I found her already there. Her orange jacket and white blouse underneath it were well matched with the weather. It was a spring day, the weather like an opening band setting the mood for a hot main performance. She was sitting on the sofa, with her back leaning against its back, reading a printout of the Global Player manual.

"Everybody at our company is satisfied with your manual for the Global Player. None of us expected to see something as wonderful as this one."

"I give credit to your wonderful product. I've done nothing. I'm just a translator."

"Too much humility becomes pride."

"But too much pride doesn't become humility. So I chose the other way around."

"You should be proud of your manual. It was that good."

"Can you tell me which part of it moved you?"

"For a start, you presented the Global Player like the Earth in explaining all of its features. I found it fascinating."

"But I think that was the product developer's idea, not mine. He designed the MP3 player in the shape of the Earth and I just made a functional interpretation of that design."

"But it was your idea to bring the Earth into the manual. That was quite unconventional. Not everyone can do that."

"They can, but they don't. Manuals exist to explain functions. My manual may be interesting to read, but I think it's only half-successful in explaining functions."

"Are you criticizing your own work?"

"I'm just saying that the world needs different kinds of manuals just as it needs different kinds of jobs. And I believe that all manuals have their own fate."

"As you said, your manual may not be perfect in explaining the product. But what we wanted was a creative manual. And that's why we commissioned your company to make one for us."

The further our conversation progressed, the weirder it became; she was paying me compliments and I was denying them. It's not every day that a client of ours praises our work as much as she did. It made me wonder if she had any hidden intentions. Rubbing her coffee cup with her fingers, she continued. "After reading the manual, I came up with a good idea. And that's what I wanted to see you about."

"I wonder what it could be."

"I'm thinking about starting a magazine of manuals. It'll feature a selection of the manuals of various products released each month. As we know, there are all kinds of manuals out there. So I thought it would be nice if someone presented them in an orderly fashion. We could also use the magazine for promoting our products, of course. What do you think about that? An interesting idea, isn't it?"

"Yes, to someone like me. But I doubt it will be a commercial success."

"I already discussed this magazine idea with my boss before I came here. And I was told to go ahead without worrying too much about making money out of it. It's all about publicity for our company."

"Why are you telling me this?"

"I want you to be the chief editor of the magazine," she said, almost whispering, slightly leaning toward me. I thought she smelled beautiful. A certain scent wafted toward me, though I wasn't sure if it was the scent of a shampoo, cosmetics, or her body. A scent so intense and powerful that for a moment I couldn't think straight. As I leaned back against the sofa, the scent followed my nose.

I accepted her offer of the chief editor position on the condition that my company would take on the overall production process, except for sales and marketing. Under the circumstances, I couldn't afford to pass up this offer, even though the project would be too big for a company of four to handle. The amount of money I was guaranteed to cover production costs for one year was large enough for me to pay off office rent and move into a larger office. We launched into a rigorous schedule for publishing the first issue of the magazine. It would have been less rigorous if I'd hired new employees, but I exploited the existing staff for maximum profit.

The first issue had a feature titled "The Manuals of the Century That Changed Our Life on Earth," and it was on this feature that we spent the most time, searching secondhand bookstores and libraries all over the country for the manuals of historically significant electronics. We even took out a newspaper ad that read: "We buy the old manuals gathering dust in your attics." The task of collecting manuals was challenging but gave us the feeling of conducting a historic mission. In a month, we collected close to five thousand manuals. While many of them were of the rarest products I'd ever seen, many of them were no better than wastepaper.

The months of preparing to make the magazine were the happiest period of my life. Even though our office had turned into a junk shop with floating book-dust causing me sneezing fits, each manual I read gave me the feeling of expanding my brain. Sorting the manuals was my job and the intern's. We sent good manuals to the bookstand on our left and bad ones to the wastebin on our right. The intern couldn't tell good manuals from bad ones without consulting me every ten minutes but finally learned the ropes after about five days.

Two months later, we finally launched *MAN-U*. This witty title for the magazine derived from the term "manual" was Quick Mouse and the intern's idea. Not surprisingly, *MAN-U* didn't receive much response, other than from an electronics newspaper, which interviewed me, and a few magazines, which ran articles on it. Goscinny seemed a little disappointed, but agreed with me that we should give the magazine at least six months before declaring it a failure. Fortunately the Global Player became a bestselling MP3 player. It was certainly good news for *MAN-U*, although it wasn't necessarily my manual that made the Global Player a success.

MAN-U grew its readership, one reader at a time. Five months later, many more readers were buying *MAN-U* and contributing scanned copies of their old manuals. *MAN-U* also earned industry recognition as more companies started sending us copies of the manuals of their new products before release. Making the magazine was fun, although it was also a lot of work and, regrettably, forced me to suspend my manual production business. But I found that the production of *MAN-U*, selecting a new feature each month and collecting manuals for the feature, was no less exciting than the production of manuals.

When I was relaxing alone on the sofa in the office after sending *MAN-U*'s seventh issue to print, waiting for the magazine to be out, Goscinny called me. I thought she'd called to see if the magazine was out, but it turned out to be about something else.

"Are you free tonight? My boss wants to invite you to dinner."

Her cheerful voice assured me that it'd be a pleasant occasion, but I was exhausted, suffering from irregular heartbeat, pins and needles in my left arm, and pain in my heels. My plan for the night was to rush home as soon as I confirmed that the magazine came out all right.

"I'll go, if you don't mind me collapsing during dinner."

"That'll prove that you've been working hard. How does seven o'clock sound?"

"Good. Will you be there, too?"

"I think so. Why? Do you mind? Do you want me out?"

"No, I want your boss out . . ."

"You're joking. Be at our office by six-thirty."

I hung up the phone and chuckled to myself. Goscinny had been deeply involved in the production of *MAN-U* from day one, visiting our office every day at my request for help. At first, she was left confused by the conversations between Park and me because she was the kind of person who took every conversation seriously. Apparently she hadn't seen many employees arguing with their boss. When we were tired from working on the first issue of *MAN-U*, we'd cheer ourselves up by making fun of Goscinny. When I growled at Park not to come to work tomorrow and Park responded that he couldn't work from home because he didn't have a PC there, Goscinny thought, in shock, that I'd just fired him. Working together for a few months, Goscinny became a good friend to all of us, as good as a fifth member of our team. Her sense of humor also improved in the process. When she was too busy with her work as a publicist to be with us, her absence weighed us down.

Once I made sure that the magazine came out all right, I took a shower in a bathhouse nearby before heading to Goscinny's office. On the bus, I tried to come up with new ideas for the feature of the next month's issue, but nothing special came to mind.

The place scheduled for our meeting was a French restaurant so posh that it immediately intimidated me. The restaurant was accessed through a garden that was nicely decorated with a dozen species of flowers and even a small pond in one corner. Two waiters at the doors bowed low to us.

"This is much too intimidating for me," I whispered to Goscinny. She just smiled. We entered the restaurant to face a vast hallway, as though we'd walked into a giant castle. With each step we took, the wooden floor of the hallway generated sound that flew up into the air like a sparrow. The room that the manager ushered us into was at the end of the hallway.

"Welcome."

On looking at the president waiting in the room, I stood dumbfounded for a moment.

"What's the matter?" asked the president.

"I'm sorry, but I thought you were a man. I don't know why I did. I apologize if I seemed too surprised."

"I see," she said, laughing. "I suppose you did because I am the president of an electronics company."

"That, too. And your name came across as a man's."

"Do you know my name?"

"Sure. You're the publisher of the magazine."

"Oh, I see. I'm sorry if I've disappointed you."

"I am sorry for having mistaken such a beautiful lady like you for a man."

The president was short and thin in every place; neck, arms and legs, everything that Goscinny, standing next to her, wasn't. Though she looked older than Goscinny, she had eyes that looked younger, and she had sharp features.

"Thank you for coming after a hard day at work." The president showed me to my seat before she took hers. There was something so formal about her gesture, but I thought that such formality reflected the sense of responsibility she had as the president of a company, the kind that a president like me would never know, who not only treats his employees like his friends but expects them to share responsibility with him.

"I've been enjoying reading *MAN-U*. I hear that its circulation is on the rise."

"Yes, but it's still losing money. I expect that it'll break even by its first anniversary."

"You don't have to be so businesslike. You're not here to give me a presentation on circulation. You must be hungry. Let's eat."

During our meal over the next hour, only small talk as light as a ping-pong ball travelled back and forth over the table. Like a pair of good sisters, the president and Goscinny talked in a low voice.

Salad, an appetizer, soup, and meat were served in that order, and none of the dishes' names rang a bell. I wanted to ask their names, but found it hard to cut into the constant stream of chatter on light subjects. I cleaned all the plates, wishing for a manual that listed the names of the dishes. They tasted delicious, tastes that told me "expensive." The wine was perfectly matched with the meat, too. By the time dessert and coffee were served, I was so full that I felt stuffed to the crown of my head.

"I invited you to dinner because I wanted to say thank you," said the president as she put powdered sugar into a cute little espresso cup that was perfectly matched with her body. My espresso was also a fine cup of coffee.

"I haven't done anything that you should thank me for," I replied.

"Let me know when you have, so I can thank you again."

"I will, so I can be treated to such fine dining again."

"Absolutely. By the way, let me ask you something. Do you decide yourself which manuals are to be featured in *MAN-U*?"

"Yes, with another employee. I remember all the manuals featured in *MAN-U*."

"What about the music box from the last issue?"

I ran the search engine in my head and it soon returned one result: a photograph from a black and white manual. It was one of the scanned pages of the product's manual, sent by a reader.

"Yes, I remember it. It was a spherical music box. Twist the ball from left to right, and it will play different music each time. It looked like a very sophisticated piece of work to me."

"You do remember it. I have that music box."

"Really? I'd like to have a look at it. The manual was so old that the photo had faded."

The president took the music box out of her purse and handed it to me. It was heavier than it looked. It resembled a basketball, but was about the size of a baseball and as heavy as a shot. Its surface was covered with a solid material, whatever it was. I tried playing the music box by twisting it, following the instructions as I remembered them. But it wouldn't budge. Nor did it play any music.

"It's not very easy, is it? Let me try." The president held the ball in her hands and twisted it in a way that I couldn't understand. Her maneuver seemed effortless. She put the twisted ball down on the table. Music started to flow out of the box. The music had a simple but sonorous melody that created the effect of playing multiple notes at the same time. The sound of music, as it escaped the ball, reached upward before it branched out in many directions and bore fruit, as though a tree had sprouted from the ball. The president, Goscinny, and I quietly admired the invisible tree standing in the middle of the round table, the sounds sprouting from the tree and falling down. Once the music box finished playing, a silence followed. The air of the room felt denser after the music. There was something still alive in the air.

"What beautiful music!" Goscinny broke the silence with her shrill voice. I wished she'd let us enjoy the silence a little bit longer.

"I couldn't play the music box until I read its manual featured in *MAN-U*. I knew it was a music box, but couldn't dare to try and play it for fear of breaking it by mistake. Now you see why I wanted to say thank you."

"How come I couldn't twist it before?"

"That's hard to explain. The key is to hold the ball in your hands and stroke it with equal force applied all over your palms. This isn't an easy feeling to describe. The point is, the more force you use, the harder it becomes to twist it. Will you try again?"

I gave twisting the ball another try, but it still wouldn't move. I stopped trying, afraid of breaking it. Goscinny didn't even try. Perhaps she couldn't stand the thought of breaking her boss's favorite item. The president twisted the ball again. It started playing different music. The air of the room felt even denser afterward.

"The music it plays varies depending on the angle of twist. Another tip I learned from the manual."

"I remember reading it, too. Where did you get such a wonderful thing? I'd like one."

The president took a chunk off of her tiramisu cake with a teaspoon and put it into her mouth. I also ate my tiramisu cake. It tasted soft and rich.

"My sister left the music box to me, but not the instructions. It wasn't much use without the instructions. It was a limited edition item, so a copy of its manual is hard to come by. It'd been sitting for ten years without playing music."

"I suppose your sister forgot to include the manual when she gave you the music box."

"Yes, I guess she tossed it once she learned the instructions."

"Why didn't you ask her to teach you?"

"I wanted to. She was in bed and I wanted to wake her up and ask her, but she wouldn't wake up. 'Please wake up and make it play music, how can I make it work?' I wanted to say to her. When my sister was in her room, she often listened to the music box. Sometimes I could also hear the music in my room. The music had the strange power to make me sleepy."

"It's a keepsake from your sister."

"What do you think it looks like?"

"I think it looks like a basketball."

"Really? That never crossed my mind."

"Or a shot, maybe?"

"You must be a sports fan. I've always thought it looks like the Earth. Look at these vertical lines. Don't they seem like longitude lines?"

Now that she mentioned it, they did. The music box certainly resembled the Earth, although I don't think that was the intention of its designer.

"Do you realize that she's telling you about the origin of the Global Player?" Goscinny said to me. "Sure, I do. I'm not that dumb, Goscinny," I wanted to say back to her. Actually, however, I had no idea. Maybe I was dumb after all, due to a lack of sleep. The president put the music box on the table. "Do you know my favorite part of your Global Player manual? Let me recite it. 'If you want to listen to the music of someone living on the other side of the Earth, plug your earphone into your desired location. It works like an old switchboard. Connect the jack to your desired country, and you will hear a song from that country. The songs that you'll hear, like crackling noise from the other side of the phone, will touch your lonely heart.' Kind of sentimental sentences, but I loved them."

I felt like a fledgling poet unexpectedly invited to a reading of his own poems. I never knew that hearing someone read my writing aloud would feel so horribly embarrassing. The paragraph the president recited was the part that took the most work in writing the Global Player manual. The most unique feature of the Global Player is that it allows the user to choose to listen to music from a certain country by plugging an earphone into that country's location on the surface of the Earth. Instead of feeling happy, as I should've, to learn that someone liked the paragraph that took me the most work to write, I just felt embarrassed.

"I could make the Global Player because I didn't know how to play the music box. I guess being without the manual can turn out to be useful."

Once the dinner with the president was over, I began to feel exhausted. After sending off the president and Goscinny, I grabbed a taxi. Less than ten minutes later my cell phone rang. It was Goscinny. "Are you going straight home?"

"No, I'd rather stay in the taxi for the next ten hours, if I could afford the fare. I'm about to collapse. What's up? You should be with your boss."

"I got out of her car. I told her that I've got something to do.

Your work for the month is done. Let's celebrate with a drink."

"Come to my taxi. Let's celebrate here. Can you afford the fare?"

The taxi driver looked at me in the rearview mirror, incredulous.

"Is it a yes or no? Be a gentleman and accept the lady's offer."

I turned to go and meet her, giving up sleep that wouldn't come anyway. Sleep doesn't come when you're too tired. When I arrived, I found Park as well as Goscinny.

"What are you doing here? I thought she'd asked me out for a date. Is this a double-date or something?"

"Just take your seat. I invited him to celebrate together as a team. It's not a date."

Our celebration lasted until 3 a.m., longer than we intended because we were excited by what Goscinny said: "My boss mentioned more investment for *MAN-U*. The details will be discussed tomorrow." Park cheered. More investment meant a raise for him. I was excited, too. It could mean a larger staff and a nicer office for me.

At 3 a.m., I went home first. What became of the two, whether they went to celebrate more, went home, or fell in love with each other and agreed to go somewhere else, I don't know. I hardly remembered anything that happened after 1 a.m.

When I woke up, it was almost sunset. What I saw upon waking up was an image of the president from last night. She was holding the music box, with a bitter smile on her face. Her image got stuck in my mind. I opened the *MAN-U* issue that featured the music box manual. The manual looked sloppy to my eyes now that they'd seen the real music box. It had few texts and relied almost entirely on illustrations to explain all of the features. Although "an illustration is worth more than a hundred words" is the general rule for manual makers, the problem was that the illustrations were poorly done. Of the ten pages of the manual, the last four were given to the company history and the contact information of the stores selling the music box on limited offer. "Press and twist the music box gently, and it will start playing music" was the most, perhaps the only, accurate part of the manual. The manual was featured in *MAN-U* not for its quality but for the rarity of the product.

Looking at the music box manual, I wondered: "How many of the manuals out there are accurate? Shouldn't I check all the products against their manuals for the credibility of *MAN-U*?" But that'd be an impossible task to complete. It'd leave me no time to work on *MAN-U*. *MAN-U* is like a code, a prayer, or speaking in tongues, and I like the way it is and I'll leave it at that for now. *MAN-U* features nothing but manuals, but who knows? It could be useful to others as it was to her."

I decided to make a new manual for the music box, thinking that I'd give it to her as a present. I considered asking Park for illustrations before I decided that the new manual might not necessarily need illustrations. My texts alone would do. As I visualized the music box, the first sentence immediately came to mind: "This music box is a seed, out of which the tree of music grows." "What do you think of this first sentence, Park?" I asked him in my mind. And I heard him say, "Not bad." "Is it kind of sentimental?" I asked the president. And I heard her say, "It's okay to be sentimental." I had the feeling of writing a love letter rather than a manual. Visualizing her face, I went on to write, or rather excavate, sentences for the manual. As I dusted the old time off the music box, and that bitter smile off her face, and the old illustration off the music box manual, sentences started to appear one by one.

Vinyl Maniac Generation

You, you, you are going to learn here, a number of ways, one, two, three, four, three, four, one, two, to transform yourself, into a DJ, D, D, DJ. While the director was rapping, I was yawning. His voice was so terrible that I couldn't stand it without a yawn. I'd been in a constant state of yawning over the past year at the academy, caused not only by the director's dull voice but, most importantly, by fatigue.

I was revolving around the same axis every day, like a record, with occasional episodes of vertigo. I worked at a record store by day, getting tired from standing. On weekends, I worked a part-time DJ job at a nightclub, still getting tired from standing. Five days a week, I took a DJ class, now getting tired from sitting. At least yawning helped me fight sleep. While I felt like I'd been going around in circles, one year had passed, miraculously. It was time to flip over the record. Not that it would stop revolving, but at least the anticipation of new songs excited me. The graduation festival was coming up next week. Once I completed it safely, I'd be awarded a professional DJ certificate from the DJ Art Research Academy.

"Going to the record stores?" DJ Koala asked me while I was cleaning up the turntable and records after class. He was a very aptly named DJ, if not a good one. One can't look at his face without a koala instantly coming to mind. To become a DJ, the first thing you need to do is name yourself. Ditch your given name and choose a name for yourself. It's cool to name yourself, whatever the name may turn out to be. I'd named myself DJ Stiff.

"Where to go today?" I asked him as I put the turntable box into the locker.

"I can't say. You tell me. I tend to find a lot of good stuff when I'm with you."

"How about going back there?"

"Where?"

"The Vinyl Cellar."

"Pulling another all-nighter?"

"It'll be quicker the second time around."

DJ Koala and I ate at a snack bar before heading to the record store we called the Vinyl Cellar. About a month earlier, we'd stumbled upon the Vinyl Cellar, ending up spending seven hours there, digging through the mountains of vinyl records. We'd obtained permission from the old storeowner, an all-night pass for digging through the heaps of vinyl records in the basement, with the doors locked, of course. We couldn't get out even if we wanted to, nor were we thinking about getting out. The place was not so much a record store as a maze, a labyrinth of the mountains of vinyl records that, if we so much as missed a step, would start tumbling down. The place stunk, too, of damp paper and musty odor unique to old vinyl records. There, DJ Koala and I'd found treasure, about thirty records. Junk to others, treasure to us. The old storeowner would open the doors the next morning to find Koala and I asleep among the vinyl records.

We arrived at the Vinyl Cellar past 11 p.m. The store would close in only one hour. Either find treasure in one hour or stay for the night. Spending the night in that basement was tough, even for vinyl maniacs. Whenever I did, I'd suffer fatigue, feeling like paper soaked in water, and smell funny all day the next day.

"Next time I'll have to come during the daytime," I'd decided. But we ended up coming at this hour anyway.

"Cut it short today. You're not going to spend the night down there again, are you?" said the old storeowner from behind us as we passed through the store on the first floor and went down the stairs. "I don't know, I can't say," replied Koala. On reaching the basement, Koala and I sniffed the air, feeling at home with the smell of vinyl.

We started digging. Digging up records takes some skills, like an eye for record design to identify the genre and a touch to the record to assess its exact condition, seeing if it's curved and/or heavily scratched. The records that pass the preliminary screening are sent to a pile for further examination. And the final selection is made based on the amount of money available. Given these skills, plus enough money, we could pick out dozens of records in one hour. Koala and I started to check out the sections that we'd missed the last time.

"I smell some good stuff over here, Stiff."

Less than five minutes into our exploration, he found a goldmine, a single stack of rare records from the sixties, the gems. This is the kind of occasional windfall I got while digging in record stores, possibly a gift from someone who needed quick cash and sold his entire album collection. Koala and I checked the records and found them in mint condition.

"With these, we could knock out everybody at the festival. Wouldn't you say, Stiff?"

"Yeah, they could save us trips to record stores for at least two years. You hit the jackpot. Take your pick first."

"No way! You brought me here. Take your pick first."

Talk about the brotherhood of DJs! Just then, we heard something from a corner, and saw the stack of records collapse, scattering them all over the floor. When the noise died down, we heard a groan and saw someone emerge from the ruins of the records. It was a man in a gray hat. Patting the dust off his jacket, the man walked toward where we stood and set about gathering up the records that we'd evenly separated into two piles.

"What do you think you are doing?" said Koala. The man said nothing.

"Can't you see we're in the middle of picking records?" said Koala, his palm covering and pressing down the records.

"I have picked these," said the man apathetically.

"What are you talking about? We've just found them. Where's the proof that these are your picks?" Koala was persistent. But the man was probably right about having picked those records himself. What else could have possibly explained the magical collection of such good records? The man stared Koala in the eyes. Koala's eyelids quivered. Ignoring Koala's question, the man resumed stacking up the records.

"Hey, mister, I said we've found them!" Koala grabbed the man by the arm. The man shook off Koala's grip in the blink of an eye and gathered about one hundred records in his arms, walking away toward the stairs. The posture in which he carried the records was well-balanced, meaning he was a professional in this field. Koala jumped over the low heap of records and stood in his way. "You crazy bastard, put them down! Can't you hear me?"

It was time for me to step in. I calmed Koala down and spoke to the man. "Forgive my friend, sir. Please understand that he's short-tempered. Let me just ask you one thing. Did you really select these records yourself?"

"Yes, I did."

"You seem to have great taste. If you don't mind my asking, are you a DJ?"

He said he wasn't. But he didn't say what he did for a living, either. Nor did he look me squarely in the eyes when he spoke. It seemed to me that he was either too shy or was trying to ignore us. In any case, we weren't going to let him go quietly.

"We are DJs. We need those records for our performance next week. Do you mind if we offer to buy them from you? We'll pay handsomely."

"What are you talking about, Stiff? Just take them from him. There's no proof anyway that that guy's picked them."

The man put down the records and set them aside. He produced his wallet from his pocket and handed me a business card on which his profession, "Collector of All Sorts of Records," was written together with his phone number.

"If you insist, I'll do you a favor and sell those records to you, but on condition."

"On condition, my ass."

I pushed Koala aside and let the man talk.

"Give me one week. I need time to listen to these records before I resell them to you."

"That's too long, I'm afraid. We need time, too, to practice for the performance next week."

"How about three days?"

"Still long, but okay, on the condition that I'll pay you whatever you paid, no more."

"Deal."

A deal was struck. Koala complained no further. He had no reason to; we'd get to buy the records we wanted at the prices we wanted, only three days later. We went to the counter with the man and made a photocopy of the list of the albums he'd bought and their prices. The man got in a car and disappeared.

I asked the old storeowner if he knew who the man was. "Well, he comes once in a while and buys a bunch of records. What he does for a living, I don't know." I wasn't surprised that the old storeowner had paid so little attention to the man, who wouldn't even haggle over prices. The customer who pays whatever's asked is welcome everywhere. As for Koala and I, we tend to spend more time haggling than selecting records. "See, it's got two scratches. Oh my God, it's even curved. I can't pay the full price for this," Koala would say, and I would chime in and say, "Uh, that's true. It's really curved." That would knock about ten percent off the price. We used this strategy while buying the thirty records the other day, and it saved us some money. But the old storeowner of the "Vinyl Cellar" didn't give us big discounts. Take-it-or-leave-it deals. Then we'd have to take it. We are the weak. Thanks to the man who wouldn't haggle over prices, we'd own secondhand vinyl records with no discounts for the first time in our lives. Well, that's something.

Koala and I skipped trips to the record stores for the next three days. They were unnecessary when we'd soon get hold of ninety-three fantastic records. We idled around for three days. Without the records, we couldn't practice. I sometimes browsed the list of the man's records, imagining the music in them. When bored, we'd chitchat by scratching the vinyl records on our respective turntables.

"*Pibibi, cheeeechickchicky, dweedweedwee, heepeepee,*" I'd say to him.

"*Tugutuguboomtsutsududuchickydoongdoong, pupubibihichickypipick, hewychickychicky,*" Koala would reply.

Although absolute Greek to others, this is a kind of communication that makes sense to us. When I distorted the sounds of a certain part, Koala responded with other sounds to match. Those sounds were as good as words to us, words that communicate one's thoughts to others. Talking was hardly necessary while we were DJing. Once, we performed the turntables for two hours on end. We didn't say a word in those two hours, but felt as if we'd been in a long conversation.

DJing requires two turntables and one mixer. Put vinyl records on the two turntables and use the mixer in the middle—specifically the lever known as the crossfader—to adjust the sounds, in a configuration that looks like this:

O_O

This is my drawing, and Koala had pinned it up on the door of his studio. Admittedly, this image was reminiscent of Koala. But the way I saw it was that it signified the relationship between him and me. One turntable connected to another by a thin line. That was Koala and me.

Three days later, we met the man at the subway station and bought the ninety three records from him. "You must've been very busy listening to all these in three days." He didn't reply. "Did you like the music?" Still no reply. We paid him. We compared each item on the photocopied list against the records. They all checked out. I gave the man a business card with my cell phone number on it, telling him to give me a call if he had any other records to sell. DJs always want new records. "Stiff, didn't you find that guy a little bit weird?" Koala said on our way back to the studio. "Did you see his eyes? They almost glowed!" But what did I care? Someone might say the same thing about our eyes if they saw us when we were performing the turntables.

Just listening to all those records in Koala's studio took us all day. As we took notes on the vinyl records with marking tape, we couldn't help but marvel at the man's taste. All great music, they were also records to be coveted by DJs. "Wow, how does he know all this music when he's not a DJ?" I wondered about it myself.

We tried putting together in our heads the bits and pieces of the music we'd heard, a process similar to putting together different pieces of glass into a pane, or working on a jigsaw puzzle. The moment all those pieces fall into place in a single large frame, the DJ's own music is born. How fast he moves the turntable or how good he is at scratching doesn't really matter. The most important qualities of a DJ are an eye for records and assembly and application abilities.

Three days before the festival, I received a phone call from the man. It was the morning after I'd stayed up all night over a few pieces of music that I couldn't put together. He said he was going to sell all of his records and asked me to come over to his storage if I was interested. Considering his taste, his storage must've been a huge treasure trove of choice records, but I didn't have that kind of money. "Don't worry about the money, just come over and take a look. I wouldn't mind if you bought just a few," the man said in a suddenly kind tone, making me as suddenly suspicious of hidden motives. But his offer was simply irresistible. "I'm not available during the day. Can I stop by in the evening?" "Okay. Give me a call in the evening." All day long, I couldn't concentrate on work. I was preoccupied with something else, having four CDs stolen in one day and cutting my hand while packaging online orders. I asked Koala to come along with me but he said he had a previous engagement. "Besides, I don't like that guy. I'm counting on you to buy a bunch of good stuff for me." The idea of going alone bothered me, but I had no choice.

The man's storage was, as I'd expected, located in a basement. It was about half the size of the Vinyl Cellar and had records stacked up in a similar but much more organized style. The sight of the records organized in the storage terrified me. "*What the . . . what kind of a man,*" I almost blurted out but suppressed myself because he was standing right next to me, watching.

"Do you think you can finish picking the records you want to buy today?" asked the man. That'd be impossible, of course. Just browsing the covers of the records would take a year. We're talking stacks of records that'd be estimated roughly at . . . no, that couldn't even be estimated.

"How much time do I have for picking the records?"

"Today."

"What happens tomorrow?"

"This place will be completely empty by then."

"Will the records be gone, all of them?"

"Yes, every single one of them. What do you say? Will you go for it?"

"Sure."

"You have until tomorrow morning. If you want to listen to the records, be my guest. There's a turntable over there in the corner."

"I can tell what I'd like without listening."

"Wow, that's great. My office is on the second floor. If you need my help, just pick up the interphone over there."

"Got it. Shall I begin?"

"As you're well aware, the door, it'll be locked." With a click, he disappeared out the door. It was 9 p.m. For a cellar, it had clean air and it wasn't cold either. It felt a little bit chilly, but I knew I'd begin sweating soon. I walked over to the turntable station: there were a run-of-the-mill turntable, a run-of-the-mill amp, and a set of cheap speakers. I took the record that was nearest to me and put it on the turntable. "I've got to take my time as much as possible." The speakers began playing music, warming up the space, as it were. I looked around the cellar. Records, records, and more records were all I saw. I divided the cellar into six sections and set up a schedule: twelve hours left until 9 a.m., two hours for each section. "It can be done, as long as my strength holds out." I started stretching, relaxing the muscles of my shoulders and hipbones. I also tried bending my back, with one of my legs resting on the speaker. The sound of the needle scratching the turntable helped me relax. I set about digging through the heaps of records. I took a ten-minute break every two hours. When two hours were up, even if I couldn't finish a given section, I didn't hesitate to move on to the next. The work turned out to be more challenging than usual. As there were simply too many records I liked, I had to raise the bar. I allowed only the records in mint condition into the cart. By 4 a.m., my throat had begun to hurt. My eyes and then my back followed. I felt like taking a break, but decided to hold on a little bit longer. Ten minutes every two hours. Rules are rules. The music was long gone. I decided to save my strength by saving trips to the turntable to play the music. The absence of music wasn't that bad; it sharpened my focus. By 7 a.m., I was tempted to give up the last section. I already had over two hundred records selected and placed in the cart, plus about thirty more, which couldn't fit in the cart, stacked up in the corner. I had enough money to buy them. With a feeling that the last section might turn out to be a treasure house of wonderful records, I brought myself to my feet again. I put a record on the turntable. My choice of music to change the mood was funk, but it failed to refresh me. By 9 a.m., all I thought was that I should get out of there as soon as possible. Out of sight, out of mind. "I have more than enough," I thought. "I'll just leave the last section unfinished."

I stacked up my selections at the door in three rows, 305 of them. One hundred of them were albums to Koala's liking, and the remaining two hundred or so would be mine. They didn't seem too many. I picked up the interphone. A few rings but no answer. I hung up and picked up the phone again. Still no answer.

Still no answer. It was 9:30 a.m. I tried calling the man's cell phone, only to get no dial tone. A red X over the phone icon, the no signal sign, had appeared on my cell's LCD screen. I felt uneasy and I felt tired. I laid myself on the sofa in the corner. With my eyes closed, I saw the covers of the records I'd looked at all night flutter like the pages of a page-a-day calendar.

The interphone woke me up. It was 10 a.m. "If I grabbed a taxi now, I could make it to work by 11," was the first thought that came to mind.

"Are you done?" said the man's voice over the interphone. I was glad to hear his voice.

"Open the door first, please. I'm freezing to death."

"Are you saying it's cold down there?"

"Have you spent a night here?"

"Have I spent a night there? How can you ask me that after seeing all those stacks of records in my cellar? I've collected every one of them with my own hands. It's taken me ten years, understand? Ten years!"

"I've picked 305 records in total. Why don't you hurry down here and we'll settle up?"

"What? 305? Jesus, 305 records? You idiot, is that all you can do down there? Is that what you think of my library? DJs . . ."

"What are you talking about? I didn't have enough time. I don't have enough money, either."

The man's disrespectful language bothered me, but I didn't think he was being so unfair because he was clearly older than me. I tried, for my part, to sound as respectful as possible. "The door is locked on the outside. I'm not the one who holds the key."

"I'll give you another hour. Make it six hundred."

"Open the door. Just open the door and talk."

The man didn't reply. I pressed CALL on the interphone but got no response.

I walked around the cellar with my cell phone in my hand. Nowhere in there did my cell phone pick up any signal. "Koala's the only one who knows that I'm here. But it's not like he knows exactly where I am. There's only one man who can open the door. That's it. Wait another hour." With no strength left for selecting the records, I grabbed the whole stack of records that was closest to me. I almost counted the records to see if they were exactly 600 before I decided against it. He had said 600 but hadn't meant a number, really. It just meant "more." Sitting on the sofa, I looked at the stacks of records, six heaps in total. Now they looked less like records and more like walls.

"Are you done?" At 11 a.m., the interphone rang again and the man's voice sounded.

"Yes, I made it six hundred."

"Exactly?

"Exactly six hundred records."

"Good job."

"Open up now, please."

"Before I do, let me ask you just one question."

My back hurt, with my shoulder joints mildly cramped and the back of my neck stiff. All I thought about was that I wanted to get out of there, whatever it might take.

"Do you think DJs are artists?"

"What do you mean?"

"You know what I mean. Are DJs artists or not? Yes or no?"

"Will you let me out if I give you the right answer?"

"I might, but can't guarantee."

"DJs aren't artists. Is that what you want to hear?"

"Forget what I want. I want to know what you think."

"I think they're artists."

"How come?"

My head was spinning like a vinyl record. "How come? That's the question I have to answer. So, how come?" I didn't know the answer.

"You're not an artist. Otherwise you'd have answered the question. My advice to you, fool, is to write down the answer and carry the note with you."

"What do you want from me?"

Anger rose up inside me but I had no means of expressing it. I couldn't use force, nor could I cry out. I felt as if my body had been enveloped in a thick film, trapped in a clear film that was neither breakable nor destroyable. The man kept silent for a while. I stared at the steel gate of the cellar. Could I break it?

"I hate DJs. Do you know why? They leave scratches on records."

"You don't know DJs. They take the best care of records."

"I was just kidding," he said, laughing. "Calm down."

"Very well, DJs aren't artists. Are you happy now?"

"Uh-oh, what happened to your sense of identity? Changing your mind so quickly? What would other DJs think of what you said?"

"Why are you doing this to me? I'm not even a DJ yet. I'm just a guy trying to become one."

"Exactly. DJs are hopeless. All they do is rip the music of others into pieces, but they think of themselves as great artists. I'm fond of people like you, people who still have potential. When I first saw you at the record store the other day, I stole a few glances at you. You seem to know quite a lot about music. Isn't that right? You think you know music, don't you?"

"I'm not sure."

"There are many ways of doing music. You can be a singer, you can be a performer, or you can be a critic. Why be a DJ?"

I pulled the sofa closer to the interphone and sat on it.

"I have a favorite song called 'Fever.' Have you heard of it? It's a famous song. I make a request whenever I'm in a bar. One day I was sitting in a bar and requested that song. Do you know what happened? The bartender played a DJ's remix version instead of the original. The DJ had totally messed up the feeling of the original and showed off all kinds of techniques instead. Shit, I can't believe they call such crap music. You have no idea how I felt then. My heart was broken, ripped apart as much as that music was. DJs like you have completely ruined my music."

"This age calls for new music."

"Don't be ridiculous. New music? Do you think that's new? Listen carefully to what DJs do. They steal some pieces from one song and some more from another, scratch here and there, remix and shuffle, copy, and then release records in their names. Makes me want to punch them in the face."

"That's how they love music in their own way. So what's your point? Are you going to kill all the DJs in the world?"

"I wish I could. I really do. I feel like locking all of them up in that cellar. I'll feed them nothing but one vinyl record a day. But it'd be like casting pearls before swine. DJs don't know music. They don't deserve it."

"You have excellent collections of music, all of them. Don't you think that someone who can tell knows music?"

"Knowing music isn't enough. You've got to feel it, instead of ripping it apart and taking advantage of the pieces . . . There is a turntable down there. Why don't you put it to good use and listen to music? Isn't it nice? Quiet. No interruptions. Lots of records . . . Feel the breaths of the artists for a change. I believe my cellar has at least a thousand fantastic records that deserve your attention. Not just 305! Can't you do better than that, you goddamned DJ?"

There was the sound of him throwing the phone and then nothing more.

Sitting on the sofa, I tried hard, but without much success, to get things straight in my head. "Why me?" Was it my fault to have met him at the Vinyl Cellar? Was this because I'd shown interest in the records the man chose? Did he see me at the nightclub where I worked? Was it that he didn't like the music I'd remixed? I had no idea. "Why me?" This question replayed itself endlessly in my head. I wasn't going to start over and pick other records. I didn't think it would make any difference which records I might choose. There was nothing I could do but wait for the man to open the door for me. Half an hour passed without the interphone ringing. I pressed the interphone and got no signal. I pushed the door of the cellar as hard as I could. The door clicked but wouldn't budge an inch. Walking around the cellar, I looked for windows or any other door. I pulled all the stacks of records off the walls to see if there was any passage behind. Nothing. The cellar was completely shut off.

I saw a crack, a very small one in the door of the cellar. I thought if I could wedge something into the crack so I could exert force, I could break the lock. The only tools available in the cellar were the records. I pulled out a record that looked solid and tried wedging it into the crack. I succeeded. With the round record in my right hand, I gave it a hard push. I felt a pain in my palm. I took off my shirt and wrapped it around my hand before trying again. I had a feeling that the lock had bent slightly. Now I used all my weight to give another push, ten, thirty, and forty pushes, to no avail. Perhaps the door was bolted. I tried in vain to remember what the door had sounded like when it'd been closed by the man the night before. All my senses had been focused on the records at that time. I broke a record into sharp pieces and then wedged one of them into the crack. I moved it up and down by inches. It was impossible to open the door. On the ceiling were a fluorescent lamp, water pipes, and a ventilator. I imagined tearing off the ventilator to reveal the hole that'd lead to a passage, only to realize that the ceiling was at least five meters high. I sat back on the sofa.

"Don't panic," I thought to myself. I assured myself that he couldn't be crazy enough to leave me in a place like this. "He's just trying to scare me for a while. Just wait a little longer." But for how long? I was hungry. I looked around the stereo for anything to eat and found only a bottle of water that was about half empty. I drank it up in a gulp. It gave me a little strength. I pulled out my cell phone again to check for a signal. I tried placing it as close to the wall as possible, but it was no use. I didn't feel sleepy but thought that I should get some sleep anyway. I imagined that everything would be back to normal by the time I woke up. I pulled the sofa right under the interphone. I closed my eyes but couldn't sleep. The air felt cold. I emptied a couple of records and pulled their jackets over my body. They didn't help much. The stinging smell of gas was getting more intense. I'd been in the cellar for sixteen hours. It occurred to me to listen to music. I put a jazz record on the turntable, cheerful songs at odds with the situation I was in. At odds or not, I needed them to calm my nerves. The sounds of the saxophone and the piano soothed me.

The florescent lamp was illuminating me like the sun at noon. The light interfered with my sleep. I turned off the lights only to realize soon that I preferred brightness. Without the clock, I couldn't have known if it was night or day. I killed time listening to music, wondering how long it'd take to listen to all the records here and thinking that given some food, being locked up here wouldn't be so bad. It was 9 p.m., but still no sounds from the interphone. Lying on the sofa, I looked blankly at the ceiling. I'd already listened to twenty records, some good and some boring.

The heaps of records piled up in the spacious cellar looked like walls. Music entered my body through one ear, and left through the other, taking my strength with it. I felt as though I were gradually turning into something I was not.

By the next morning, I'd been left too weak even to walk toward the turntable. The last piece of music I'd played was echoing in the cellar. I kept hearing the voice of the female singer in the air. My mind was blank. I stayed awake almost the whole night, except for a few hours of catnapping. I felt a pain in my heart. "What could Koala be doing? Is he looking for me, or preparing for the festival?" The thoughts in my head wafted like smoke. Certain thoughts kept occurring to me, but none of them were complete. By the afternoon, the echo in the air was gone. Only the buzz remained in my ears. I had no idea what it was.

By the third day, I'd fallen into a weird state of hallucination. Briefly closing my eyes, I'd see strange objects. "This is what happens when I die," I thought for a moment. I thought I heard the sounds of music from somewhere. "Someone's probably put a new record on the turntable. Who could that be? There's no one else here." There were footsteps, faintly at first but then in a crescendo. With thumps, they were rocking my head. And there were knocks on the door. A man's face came into view, and disappeared.

When I opened my eyes again, I found myself lying in a hospital bed. I saw an IV and Koala's face next to it. He was smiling. I wanted to say something to him but didn't know where to begin.

"Awake at last," said Koala. Stammering, I asked him what had happened. But Koala knew nothing, except for the fact that I'd been found collapsed in a certain basement.

Three days later, I reported myself to the police. They asked me what'd happened. I asked them what'd happened. The police produced a piece of paper from a file and showed it to me. It was a WANTED poster, with a seemingly old photograph of the man and a list of his charges written underneath: illegal record production, fraud, etc. Apparently he'd been selling CDs that he'd produced from the vinyl records in the cellar. Considering the size of his record collection, I could imagine the scale of the production. Tracking down the man's online site, the police had located his cellar and made a raid on the place, where they found me collapsed on the sofa. I recounted to the police the events that'd led up to my collapse on the sofa. It wasn't an easy thing to do. "He said he hated DJs." Who would buy that? Anyway, I managed to convince them at least that I had nothing to do with the man. "Why me?" I wanted to address that question to the police, but that was the same question they wanted to ask me. The man was at large. His CD production equipment was found, but not until he was gone.

I had to quit my part-time job at the record store. I wasn't in normal condition, either physically or mentally, though I had nothing one could call serious aftereffects. I sometimes heard strange music in my ears, and broke out into a cold sweat whenever in an elevator. I also quit the DJ academy. Since I couldn't participate in the graduation festival, I couldn't receive a DJ certificate. Nor did I want to, even if it was offered to me. Fortunately, Koala finished the festival successfully. With two turntables and a mixer, he'd driven the audience to the point of swooning, or so he told me. I was in bed at the time. Koala said he'd have cancelled his participation in the festival if I hadn't been found. I'd have done the same for him. Koala became a hot DJ after the festival, receiving offers from many nightclubs and even an offer for a record deal. "I wish you could join me," Koala said, but I wasn't the least bit interested in joining him. Koala performed so much that he began to suffer from Carpal

Tunnel Syndrome (CTS), characterized by numbness in the fingers and palms, a common occupational hazard for DJs. Koala invited me to all of his performances. During a performance at the DJ Art Research Academy, he called me up to the stage and introduced me to the audience. "This is my teacher, such a great DJ." He told me to give them a turntable performance, but I couldn't do it. I almost felt sick looking at the turntable turning. I just gave a bow to the audience and stepped down from the stage. Koala had a knack for driving people wild. His hands were manipulating the turntable faster, creating complex beats at will. He also did a rap, imitating the director, in front of the students. *You think DJs are pounders? A thump, a thud, a thump, a thump, a thud, a thump, no beats, no secrets, no talent, no luck, you come to a place like this in the middle of night for a bang, thumps, thumps, DJs don't just turn the record, if you want to, want to do what you're told not to, not to, then don't be a DJ, shuffle, shuffle two pieces of music, do it well, or just go home and shuffle flower cards.* His voice and tone almost exactly matched the director's and the audience burst out laughing. I laughed, too. For a very brief moment, I envied Koala.

The biggest trouble was that I couldn't sleep well. When I closed my eyes, I'd see a giant fluorescent lamp fall down and hear distant footsteps. I sent all the vinyl records in my room to Koala's studio. The sight of any vinyl record was a horrifying reminder of the cellar. When I lay on my bed and looked at the ceiling, I'd hear the man's voice. I often heard the man say, "I'll give you another hour. Make it six hundred." I tried to erase that voice with other music in my head. But there was no music left in my head.

Six months after the incident, I received a phone call from the police. The man had been arrested. I hesitated but eventually agreed to come to the police station. When I arrived, he was under interrogation. I saw him through the one-way glass. "Do you admit your charge of illegal record production?" "Illegal? My only crime, if there is one, is that I've spread beautiful music to the world." "You made money from selling those CDs." "I only charged the fair price. I need money to make beautiful music." "You keep saying beautiful music. What is it anyway?" "It's music with soul. Not like that trashy music flooding the world today." "By the way, why did you lock him up?" "Who?" "Don't you remember locking him up?" "I don't know what you're talking about." He didn't seem to remember. His eyes appeared to plead ignorance. I wanted to see no more of him. I wanted to get out of there.

I headed for Koala's studio but Koala wasn't there. He was probably at a party or a nightclub performance. It was Friday night. Koala had the ninety-three vinyl records from the man neatly stacked up in the corner. To Koala, those records, which had made him a star, were as good as treasure. Squatting down on the floor, I flipped through the records one by one. Is each of these songs really unique music in the world? Was the music of these artists created out of nothing? I don't think so. There's nothing new under the sun. Someone influenced by someone else, who had been influenced by someone else, who had been influenced by yet someone else, makes a drawing of his own on top of those many existing sketches. The drawing by that someone, in turn, will serve as a sketch for someone else. We're all connected to a number of invisible strings. That makes all of us DJs to a certain degree; me, Koala, the man, and yet someone else, all of us. Looking at the records, I felt a growing resentment against the man. The only way to get even with him would be to become an established DJ, and then present him with the record released under my name. I wanted to see the man stare back at me, looking annoyed, when he received my record. I picked two records and put each of them on one of the two turntables. I turned on the power and pumped up the volume. I had mild dizziness, but it wasn't unbearable. With the mixer, I mixed the two different pieces of music from the two turntables into a single sound. As in the 'O _ O' drawing I had made for Koala, I connected the beats flowing out of the two pieces of music into one. The cacophony of different sounds turned into a harmony with the use of my hands. The beat flowing out of the speakers and the headphones filled the studio, a beat that I hadn't felt in a long time. My heart raced. This beat is me. I am a DJ.

The Library of Musical Instruments

"Dying as nobody is unfair." This phrase flashed through my mind the moment my body was hit by the car and flung into the air. Instantly, every picture around me collapsed and every sound was muted. A complete isolation. I saw nothing, heard nothing, and remembered nothing. I just had the feeling of being slowly sucked into a large capsule, head first. "Dying as nobody is unfair." This phrase shielded my head like a thick helmet. Landing with a thud, I blacked out.

I survived, thanks to that phrase. Nobody believed me, but it was really that phrase shielding my head like a helmet that saved me. Not until then did I realize that the power of thinking could put a body in thick armor, and that it was possible to escape death if one tried. Lying in the hospital, encased in white plaster from head to toe, looking like the mythical yeti of the Himalayas, I chewed on that phrase all day long. It was stuck in my mind, although my memories of how I'd come to get hit by the car or how high up in the air my body had been flung had been completely erased. When I closed my eyes, I'd see a white wall with that phrase written all over it. When I opened my eyes, I'd find the wall gone but that phrase thrashing like fish in my head. I was alive, always with that phrase. Before I went to sleep, I'd recite that phrase as if it were a charm that'd keep me alive. Every time I woke up, I'd find myself alive.

N, still my girlfriend then, kept music on while I was in bed. When I told her about that phrase thrashing in my head, she teased, "I can see you hit your head really hard," and then upped the volume. Sonata, concerto, symphony, and back to sonata. Music played without a break. I was exposed to it twenty-four hours a day without knowing who was playing what. "Music's the best therapy for broken bones," she said, although the perceived effect of music on my body was more like squeezing my flesh than healing my bones. Music had another effect on me; it definitely made me feel alive. I almost felt in my bones those musical notes that were floating around in the hospital room air.

I stayed in the hospital for three months before I could walk again. Despite my left shinbone, bent like a bow, I could walk fine. As soon as my legs could function, I visited the scene of my accident. I felt I needed to be there, although I had nothing to retrieve or check out. I combed the ground, almost convinced that I could spot that phrase lying around. No trace was found, of course. Not even a shard of glass. I realize now that I was conducting a kind of ritual, perhaps out of my desire to visit the place where I could've perished and to show that place that I was still alive.

My post-accident life would be wrought with many changes. For a start, I'd quit my job. When I told my boss, and nobody else, about that phrase, he wouldn't accept my resignation, laughing it off. "Don't be ridiculous. Just give yourself some time to rest and get back to work. When it comes to life's unfairness, I know a lot more than you do." I sensed a hint of jealousy in his voice. He asked me what I was going to do for a living. I had nothing to say. Once I quit my job, I'd started drinking. It was the worst habit I could've chosen when my body was still recuperating, but I couldn't put my body to sleep without intoxicating it first. I knew I was supposed to be doing something that help me avoid dying as nobody, but I didn't know where to start. I bought myself three cases of the cheapest white wine I could find at a large discount store and went on to drink them one bottle at a time every night. The astringent taste, which at first made me regret that I hadn't gone for more expensive wine, eventually grew on me. By the time I almost finished a bottle I'd redden all over and start feeling drowsy. It was a warming-up process, I reassuringly explained to my girlfriend, that was necessary to prepare myself for sleep, and there was nothing to worry about. What it really was, however, as it was obvious even to me, was an early symptom of alcoholism. But drinking had positive effects. It'd scrape that phrase off me. It'd also rid me of the anxiety that I might not wake up alive the next morning. That alone was worth it.

My routine of uncorking a new bottle of wine and drinking myself to sleep every night in the corner of my room would've continued if I hadn't passed by the music shop in the discount store one month after I started drinking. Not that I think there's anything wrong with that lifestyle. In hindsight, I can see that everything was part of a process. The car accident caused that phrase to flash through my mind, on account of which I started drinking, on account of which I found the music shop. When seemingly unrelated events are connected in a line, it changes your life. That line, I suppose, when extended, is what constitutes a person's life.

Having consumed all three cases of white wine within a month, I headed to the discount store for more. On the escalator leading down to the basement, I noticed a large mirror in front and turned my face to the right to avoid my own reflection, too terrible to face. My gaze met the flashy Christmas tree decorations twinkling over the railings, which told me that Christmas was coming. About a quarter of the way down to the basement on the escalator, I noticed a piano in the music shop on the first floor. I still remember the amount on the price tag placed on the keyboard. The price seemed affordable, although it would've seemed steep if not for the settlement money and severance pay still left untouched in my bank account. Next to the piano was a lineup of a guitar, a violin, and other musical instruments that looked like toys. Standing on the escalator and gazing up at the instruments, I was reminded of my girlfriend. She was running a small violin school with a friend. Recorded performances of famous artists always made her sigh in frustration. She said she envied the sounds of the violin, not the excellent skills of the artists. "You play your music with your soul, not with your instrument," I'd said in a dumb attempt to comfort her. But what knowledge of music did I have that would qualify me to say something like that? I went back up to the first floor and entered the music shop.

As it turned out, the violin was ridiculously cheap. I didn't understand the price until I examined the instrument carefully. The violins selling at the music shop were the kind of instruments that one could only hope, but never expect, would actually make sounds. I forgot about the violins and went home after buying myself a case of wine.

The next day, I told my girlfriend that I'd like to buy her a violin. She jumped at my offer and immediately took me out to shop. I dreaded how much her violin would cost. At the same time, I thought I wouldn't mind if her violin cost me a fortune and drained my bank account. My money would be better spent on her violin than on my wine. Who knows? Maybe I'd figure out what to do with my life when my money was gone.

When I set out to shop for what I thought would be a random violin with a high price tag, I didn't expect that window-shopping for musical instruments with my girlfriend would be as much fun as it turned out to be. Although my legs weren't exactly in perfect condition to be walking around in music shops, I was happy just to be alive and able to walk with her. Talking with her, I found myself eager to learn an instrument.

"Which instrument?"

"How about piano? I've got big hands."

"Long fingers help, but large hands don't. They're prone to hit two keys at once. Did you ever learn piano when you were young?"

"Never."

"How come?"

"I was busy learning Taekwondo."

"I see. I guess that's more useful in life."

"Not really."

"I see."

"I like the sounds of the cello. Is it difficult to learn cello?"

"How about the violin?"

"Are you going to teach me?"

"Why not?"

"I don't like the sounds of the violin. They're depressing."

"Wait until you appreciate their depth."

"The deeper, the more depressing."

"Okay. Violin or cello, it's your choice . . ."

Even though I told her I wanted to learn an instrument, I wasn't sure if I could actually put myself through it. I had no musical talent whatsoever, and I saw no use in learning music. After all, my mind was only set on avoiding dying as nobody and doing something so great that it would leave my mark on history.

The last shop we stopped by that day was her favorite one, which also had the largest collection of instruments. Musica, as the shop was called, might as well have been a museum for its neatly organized collection of all kinds of instruments. I could see that a lot of effort had gone into organizing the instruments, whatever the organizing system may have been.

"Welcome back, miss. Used ones are out of stock, though."

"I'm not here for used ones today, sir. Don't you see I'm with my patron over here? He's a crash-for-cash scammer and he's just pulled off a big one. He said he'd spend that money on buying me the coolest violin in the world."

"Then I'm not selling. No bad money for instruments."

"Would they make bad sounds?"

"More distorted sounds, I'd say."

"Great. That's exactly the kind of sound I want."

The mustached boss and my girlfriend sounded like a well-trained team who'd spent a long time studying humor together. Although I'd just found out from her that my profession was crash-for-cash scammer, I liked how she'd put it, the way it made me feel as though I wasn't actually hurt and the accident had been a dream.

The mustached boss struck me as a man who had nothing to do with music, but his first impression wasn't bad. The moment I laid my eyes on him, I was enchanted by his mustache. The thought that his mustache might be the desperate attempt of a man who had nothing to do with music to look like an artist added to its charm. Judging by what he'd tell me later, my guess was half-right. His mustache would change its shape from triangle to straight line whenever he wore a grin while bantering with N. His repeatedly contracting and expanding mustache was so fascinating that I spent quite a long time observing it at first.

"This is my boyfriend." She finally introduced me to him when she decided they'd swapped enough jokes. He smiled, straightening out his mustache again. They carried on with their conversation, mostly in jargon that sounded Greek to me. I killed time by playing with the instruments, tapping on the keys of the piano sitting in the corner or plucking the strings of the cello. Before I knew it, I sensed a slightly excited tone in the voice of the boss.

"That's a really stupid categorization, if you ask me."

"Well, but everyone's using it. Hard to change it now."

"Tell me what you think, miss. Does the term stringed instrument fit the description of the violin?"

"Well, the violin does have strings."

"Does that make *janggu* a stringed instrument, too? It's got pinched strings."

"They're not used in making sounds, Mr. Sophist."

"What are you talking about? They control sounds."

"But you don't vibrate its strings to make sounds with *janggu*."

"Hit *janggu*, and its strings will definitely make some sounds. Any sounds. At least some mosquito-buzzing sounds, perhaps?"

"Do you call those sounds music?"

"What about the piano, then? Is it a stringed or a percussion instrument? Is it a stringed instrument because it has strings? Or is it a percussion instrument because we hit it? Don't pluck the strings of the violin, or it would make the violin a percussion instrument, not a stringed one."

While my eyes were facing the keys of the piano, my ears had detached themselves and moved closer to their conversation. I found the mustached boss's argument intriguing. The conversation between the two, who seemed like employees of the Humor Research Institute, had turned into a panel discussion on musical instruments. Their conversation was interrupted as a customer walked in to pick up his serviced instrument. I put my hand on the keyboard, stretching my thumb and ring finger as far as I could to see how far apart the two keys might be that I could reach at the same time. With my fingers too tense, I ended up pressing the keys too hard. The ding echoed across the quiet shop. I could almost feel their collective gaze, but I kept mine fixed on the keys, feigning ignorance. To my relief, the mustached boss and my girlfriend said nothing. As soon as the customer left, their conversation resumed.

"Anyway, I think it's ridiculous to label instruments percussion, strings, and wind. I've played enough instruments myself to know that many of them don't fit any of those categories. If there are so many exceptions, then the categories might be wrong in the first place. What do you think, mister?" The mustached boss suddenly addressed me, as if he knew all along that I was listening in.

"Me? Well, I . . . don't know anything about music."

"I'm not asking you about music. I'm asking you about categories."

I closed the cover of the piano and walked toward the display case at which the two were standing.

"I've been thinking while listening to you talk, and I actually thought it was kind of strange."

"What's strange?" asked my girlfriend, with a look that said she couldn't believe I had broken into the conversation.

"I'm just curious. What does 'wind' mean, as in wind instruments?"

"It means you make sounds by breathing wind into a pipe."

"Then, I gather 'wind' refers to a tool for making sounds. As for the strings, you make sounds by vibrating the strings, right? In this case, sounds are generated directly from the strings. So categorically speaking, I guess the strings are a bit different from the winds. And 'percussion' as in percussion instruments means to hit, so I guess their category also differs from that of the winds or the strings altogether."

"Exactly. Well summed up, mister."

"You made sense to me. You never sounded smarter." My girlfriend nodded, pursing her lips. It was amazing how smoothly my thoughts on the categories of musical instruments had started coming out of my mouth, well organized, like a blanket folding itself up neatly, although I'd never considered such a topic before in my whole life. The compliments from the two gave me a brief moment of elation that I enjoyed immensely, though it's embarrassing to admit now. The three of us could hold such a conversation only because none of us were aware that musicologists weren't as dumb as we assumed they were. Three months later, I'd learn that scholars had already come up with different categories for musical instruments: aerophones for the winds, idiophones for percussion, and chordophones for the strings. Nevertheless, I'm still proud of myself for having quickly figured out what was wrong with the three names that I hadn't considered before, especially when many people are still using the terms—strings, percussion, and winds—without questioning their meaning.

I couldn't have been more thrilled at the compliments from the two, as though I were the one who'd discovered some new truth, like I was the one who'd figured out for the first time that the Earth was round. The mustached boss, my girlfriend, and I chatted for two hours. The other two did most of the talking while I listened. But at least my comments on the categories of instruments had earned me an official invitation to the conversation. Eighty percent of the conversation revolved around music, and personal stories were thrown in occasionally. The mustached boss said that running Musica was becoming increasingly difficult, and my girlfriend said that the parents of students at her school were becoming increasingly rude. When the story of my accident was brought up after all these complaints about how things were getting worse, the mustached boss's eyes opened wide. It's definitely exciting to hear the story of someone else's car accident, especially when it's told by the one who survived the accident. Except that I didn't have much to say. "I was taking the crosswalk on my way home from work, when I was hit by a car. I don't quite remember the rest." "Is that all?" The mustached boss frowned. Reluctantly, I added the story of that phrase, that I was drinking a bottle of white wine every night, and that I couldn't go to sleep without drinking.

"What exactly does dying as nobody mean, anyway?"

"To be honest, I don't really know either. It could be a code, in a way, or it could just be gibberish."

"That's it. I've always thought that phrase was a little bit weird. Whenever you talk about it, I doubt it's even grammatical."

"But that phrase, there are moments when it becomes a single mass and takes control of my head. It turns into something liquid and floods my head. Then I can't breathe. I feel like I'm dying, like I won't be able to breathe ever again, like I can never be born again, like I might be someone else even if I was born again. That's what it makes me feel. A feeling you'd get before you drown. How can I not drink?"

"Does drinking help, though?"

"I replace the liquid flooding my head with drinks, putting a stop to my brain."

"Honey, why don't you go to see a doctor?"

"What should I tell him? My brains are drowning, so please drain them?"

"No, you should see a psychiatrist."

"Forget it. This isn't the kind of problem they could fix."

"Did you have to quit your job?"

"Considering my condition, I couldn't stay in my job, could I? I need some time off to put my thoughts together."

"What an idiot. If you died working, it wouldn't be dying as nobody. But if you died now, it'd really be dying as nobody."

"I hope you don't mind me saying this to you, since we've just met, but how about giving working here a try?"

"Working at Musica?"

"Business here isn't going well, so I have started another one. But instead of folding this shop, I was thinking about hiring a clerk. I think the job will suit you. Just consider it a pastime. What do you say? You said you wanted to learn an instrument. We have weekly lessons for piano, cello, viola, and violin. You're free to take any of them, too. Free of charge."

"I don't think I'm qualified. I'm too old for a part-timer. And I don't know anything about instruments."

"Yes, you do. You've just demonstrated your keen insight into percussions, winds, and strings. Consider my offer, please."

"Do you think my appearance fits the job of selling instruments?"

"Do you think it takes looks to sell instruments? You're funny. You look good enough to sell instruments. Don't worry."

The next day, I gave the mustached boss a phone call to accept his offer. I told him that I didn't need paychecks because I might have second thoughts, but the mustached boss was very insistent. So I eventually agreed to a minimal wage, plus free instrument lessons. He said if I picked an instrument I wanted to learn, he'd lend me one for free. The purpose of my decision to work at Musica was to neglect myself. I just wanted to let myself go with the flow of whatever might happen to me, to watch from a distance as my life skewered new events one at a time.

My part-time job at the music shop turned out to be unexpectedly fun. When my job was to serve customers and there were at most three customers coming in per day, mostly window-shoppers, I didn't have much to do. When parents walked in with their children and pestered me with questions about which instrument would be good for their children, I'd trot out what was written in my boss's instructions: "I'm sorry, but my boss is not in right now." "It's frustrating that I can't really help the customers," I said uneasily to the mustached boss, who said that it was okay. He was right. Most regulars of Musica placed orders directly with the mustached boss when they needed instruments. So all I had to do was to hand over the delivery to the customers when they came in for pickup and help them pay the balance. Still, feeling that I should educate myself enough at least to tell one instrument from another, I started reading The Illustrated Book of Musical Instruments in my spare time. Occasionally, I sold supplies, too, like guitar strings and scores.

Although I had done my share of music listening in the hospital, enough to have almost damaged my eardrums, listening to music at the shop was an entirely different experience. The presence of instruments made all the difference, the way the presence of the film director sitting next to you in a preview would make a difference to your experience of his film. When listening to a piano sonata, I was placed under the illusion that someone was sitting at the piano and playing the piece. There were an infinite number of sounds an instrument could make, and my mind, in responding to each of them, was also obviously in a different state each time.

It was strange that my girlfriend's live violin performance for me on her occasional visits to the shop wouldn't arouse the same feeling. Neither would the CDs from the shop that I brought home for listening. Once, I tried recording her live performance. "Now that you've got yourself a nice new violin," I told her, "why don't you try to give a great performance with it?" So she did, really pouring herself into her performance, as if she were making a real record. Whenever I was alone at the shop listening to that recording, I would feel exactly as she must have felt.

As for the instrument lessons, I gave them up after two weeks.

As the lessons were conducted mainly in a small room in the corner of the shop, it was hard for me to take the lessons and run the shop at the same time. Running the shop, though it didn't serve many customers, still demanded my attention. I was halfway through learning how to hold the cello bow when I called it quits. I was still happy, content with listening to music while beholding the instruments.

In two months, I became knowledgeable enough to tell the differences among a wide variety of instruments and to help customers with simple tips. I made such rapid progress in my clerkship that it prompted the mustached boss to say wishfully, "If only you were a little bit younger, I would've made you a regular employee." In three months, I was reading *A Music Shop's Guide for the Effective Arrangement of Musical Instruments*, which I'd checked out from the library, making a mental plan of how the shop should be rearranged. It was from the same book that I'd learn what a stupid idea it was to group musical instruments into strings, winds, and percussions. But I didn't quite like the scholars' categorization either. "The biggest problem with categorizing instruments," I thought, "is the possibility of denying potential new instruments." I wanted to try my own categorization of instruments. Instead of following the boss's organization of instruments, based on how they made sounds, I grouped together instruments with similar tones. Violin and cello, for instance, shared a similar mechanism for making sounds but had completely different tones, so I separated them in location on the floor. By that time, with the mustached boss's other business making rapid progress, I'd been put almost completely in charge of running the shop, at liberty to move the instruments around and experiment with different floor arrangements.

At some point, I found myself playing with the instruments, recording their sounds. I used a piece of computer software to store and organize the sound clips in folders on the PC. It was a slow process. To record the sounds of many unfamiliar instruments, I had to rely on *The Illustrated Book of Musical Instruments* for instructions on how to play them. I was recording myself playing *with* the instruments, not necessarily *playing* them, but it was still a lot of work. Any given instrument had at least thirty different tones. With about six hundred types of instruments available in the shop, I had on my hands at least eighteen thousand different kinds of sounds to sample. Although I can't claim that my sampling covered the entire spectrum of sounds of a single instrument, at least I tried as many methods of making sounds as I could: scratching, scraping, beating, plucking, petting, or pinching. I believe that my ears have grown as sensitive as they are now thanks to all the sound sampling work I did at that time. If I hadn't summoned all the senses distributed across my body and concentrated them on my eyes and ears, I couldn't have identified and organized those different sounds.

I had so much fun with the sound sampling project that I practically moved myself into the shop, sleeping on the cot I set up in the music lesson room. As I stayed up late into the night recording the sounds of instruments until daybreak, my drinking habit naturally disappeared. My girlfriend teasingly called me "terminally paranoid," apparently too appalled at a kind of seriousness in me that she hadn't seen before to even try to talk me out of it. She left me and the reason was, not necessarily entirely but decisively, in my opinion, what she thought was my paranoia. I was working on a goal that was pointless, contributing nothing to world peace, making no money, and taking eternity to finish. To me, the project was like a space mission you go into, fully aware that there would be no return trip, or like a dive you make without an oxygen tank for your return trip. I found the impossibility of finishing it the most appealing aspect of the project.

Her decision to love another man was unfortunate for me, but I had no choice. I believe that everything was just part of a process, but that was *my* process that I couldn't force on *her*.

Once I'd almost used up the money in my bank account by buying myself a piece of recording equipment, a computer, and sound-editing software, I set aside an amount from my monthly salary to spend on another, more easy-to-use piece of recording equipment. As if recording the sounds of instruments wasn't enough, I began recording all kinds of sounds around me: the footsteps of customers, coughs, the squeaking mice living above the ceiling of the shop, my hand pounding on the wooden table, the washing machine in action, and boiling water. I hit the record button whenever I encountered any audible and recordable sounds, without any plans whatsoever to do anything with them. I recorded as naturally as I breathed.

One day, I was in one of my usual sound-recording sessions in the music lesson room at the shop, recording myself playing with the Ghanaian frame drum. This frame drum was, unlike a normal drum, in the shape of a large rectangular tray, and playing it turned out to be a stunt that involved placing the instrument on the floor at a 45-degree angle and then juggling between my heels controlling the pitches and my hands hitting the drum. I was moving around my heels recording various sounds of the drum when the boss opened the door of the room. I may have been totally deafened by the drum sounds. That's why I didn't realize he was there until he said, "What is all this? What are you doing?"

This startled me into dropping the frame drum onto the floor. The microphone stand on the floor was knocked over, making a thunderous noise. I knew I was supposed to explain to the mustached boss the situation he'd found himself in, but I was dumbfounded by all the noise. Without closing the door,

Without closing the door, the boss took a look around the room crowded with the cot, assorted recording equipment, and a few instruments waiting for their turns.

"You look busy. Should I come back some other time?" Amidst all the confusion, the boss still managed to joke.

"I'm sorry. I didn't even know you'd come in."

"I've just arrived from the airport, stopping by on my way home. Thought I'd just check to see if the instruments were surviving this cold weather. Would you like a glass of wine?"

I made a shopping trip to the nearby convenience store for two bottles of white wine, a box of crackers, and paper cups. It was time for me to tell the boss what I'd been up to. The more I explained what I was doing and why I'd started doing it, the more obscure my story seemed to become. I was afraid that it was going to sound like a very long and boring joke.

"Sounds like fun."

"Makes me lose track of time, actually. I'm not sure what I can do with it, though."

"Do you have to do anything with it?"

"I've recorded about eight thousand sound clips. Isn't it crazy to make eight thousand files just for the fun of it?"

"I think I could do something crazier, as long as it's fun."

"You do?"

Maybe the weather was so cold or the refrigerator at the convenience store was running well. The white wine felt very cold. I wrapped my hands around the paper cup. The wine-soaked paper cup had become soggy.

"Could you run this place for me for one year?" asked the mustached boss, pouring wine into my cup.

"Run Musica? Are you going somewhere?"

"I have business that needs me overseas for a while. I'll have to sell this place, but don't have time for that. So it'd be great if you could either run it or sell it for me. If you think you could make enough money to cover the expenses and your salary, I'd prefer you keeping the shop running."

"You're asking me to either quit now or never for a year. Am I right?"

"Yeah, sort of. Even if you decide to quit now, I'd like you to stick around for a while until the shop is sold. I'll make it up to you with a fat severance pay."

"Let me give running the shop a try."

To my surprise, it took me less than a minute to make such an important decision. My decision was motivated by many factors: the fear of suspending my ongoing project; the joy of indulging myself in different instrument organization ideas; and whatever else was running through my head.

"You seem so sure about yourself. That's so unlike you. I thought you were going to say, 'Well, do you think my appearance fits for the job of selling instruments for one year?'" The boss's imitation of my voice made me burst into laughter.

"But what if I stole all these expensive instruments and ran off?" I asked, still laughing.

"That's exactly what I want you to do. Run off with the instruments, so I can claim my insurance money. Go ahead and do it, please. If I find even a single instrument around when I come back, you're fired."

"Are you serious?"

"Of course not. You should learn some humor. Once you get used to it, your life will be easier."

The second cup of wine was at the right temperature. I was unconsciously tearing the brim off the paper cup. A very old habit of mine.

"As I walked in earlier, I noticed some change in the arrangement of the instruments."

"Yes, I've made it to pass time. I'll put them back the way they were."

"Only if you want to. Remember you're the boss here now for one year. I noticed something about you today that makes you right for this shop. I'm just a trader. Traders, you know, have only one goal in life: buy low and sell high. And I like that you're not a trader like I am. But be careful. Push yourself too hard, and you'll burn yourself out. You can't expect to sustain this kind of lifestyle for more than six months."

The next day, the boss came back to give me a list of instructions for running the shop. It was written down neatly on a small piece of paper: how to order instruments, how to contact the instrument repair service agent, where to call for help in an emergency, and so on. That little note alone could tell us what kind of person the mustached boss was.

"This should be enough to get you through one year, three even."

"You sound like you're leaving me on a remote island."

"Why? Are you scared?"

"Not really."

"Well, sorry if I scared you. Do you sleep well these days?"

"My brains are clean. It's amazing. I guess the sounds of instruments have helped drain them completely."

"Good. The sounds of instruments are better than drinks. Your story got me thinking. About that phrase, you know? How did it go again, exactly?"

"It goes, dying as nobody is unfair."

"Right. Rings true to me when I think about it. I'd feel it was unfair, too. If I were a writer, or filmmaker, or politician, or great inventor, or composer, then I'd be remembered. That's what that phrase implies, isn't it? Like a wish that I'd be remembered."

"I'm not sure. It might, though."

"If that's the case, don't worry. I'll remember you."

"Thank you."

I have no idea why I said "Thank you" when I knew that making a joke like "I'll remember you, too, boss" or just smiling would've served me better. At my "Thank you," the boss grinned, straightening out his mustache.

"While you're changing the arrangement, why don't you change the name of the shop, too? Musica . . . it's such an old-fashioned name, isn't it?"

"I like it. Simple, easy to remember, decent."

"How does 'The Unfair Music Shop' sound? You and I both lead an unfair life."

That was the last joke between the boss and me before he left. The next day, I took time off of recording to consider shop makeover, how the instruments should be rearranged to add a new touch to the shop. It was around that time that my girlfriend broke up with me. I felt as though I'd really turned into an isolated island. To take my mind off of everything, I focused myself on work, redecorating the music lesson room, adding more lessons, trying a completely new floor plan for the instruments, hanging a large musical instrument classification chart on the wall, setting up a music listening room with headphones in the corner, and serving the customers free coffee. All of this was intended to both help Musica generate more profit and make it a place bustling with people, not an isolated island.

The Musical Instrument Library Project was born solely on account of one girl. She was a middle school girl taking violin lessons on Wednesdays. One day, she approached the counter and spoke to me. "Sir, do you have an instrument called the sitar?"

"Not right now. Are you interested in buying one? Do you want me to place an order for you?"

"No, I just wonder what it sounds like."

"I see. Hold on a minute. Let me find a record of a sitar performance for you. It's got to be somewhere around here . . ."

"No, not a performance record. I just need the sounds of the instrument."

"You mean you just want to hear its sounds?"

"I read in a book that the most forlorn sound in the world is the sound of gently plucking a sitar string in an empty room."

"I see. That might be true."

I was going to just turn the girl away until I realized that I did have some sitar sounds.

"This is a recording I made of sitar sounds. You can listen to it, if you want."

"I can? Can I borrow it, too?"

"I'll make a copy on a cassette tape for you. It'll play the sounds of plucked sitar strings. But remember, this is just a recording of sounds, not a performance, okay? No great music or anything."

I wondered how she'd like the sounds, but my expectations weren't high. If anything, she'd be disappointed. After all, what she'd hear wasn't music but a five-minute stream of the instrument's strange sounds. But I was wrong. The girl came back the next day. "I loved it. It taught me what it was like to be forlorn."

"It did?"

"Absolutely."

So began the Musical Instrument Library Project. Not that it started off under that name, of course. Nor did I expect to see it grow into something this big. The beginning was humble. My first idea was to make the sounds of instruments available in the music listening room. I called a former coworker of mine and discussed my idea with him. "It sounds to me like a jukebox," he said. "Yeah, something like that," I replied. My ex-coworker agreed to write me a simple program for a modest fee that'd be his pocket money. He and I worked on the program, and I purchased a dedicated computer on which to install it. The expenses were covered by my monthly salary.

Less than a month after its completion and release, the Musical Instrument Sound Jukebox had become a famous attraction, not just of Musica but of the whole music shop district. The best thing about the Musical Instrument Sound Jukebox was its check-out feature: choose a desired instrument, press the download button, and the sounds of the selected instrument would be recorded on the minidisc player connected to the computer. It was also possible to download the sounds of multiple instruments at once.

People checked out the sounds of an instrument for a variety of reasons. Some wondered how a certain instrument sounded, like the girl who was the Musical Instrument Library's first customer. Others wanted to expose their children at home to the sounds of instruments. For some, listening to the sounds was much more effective than listening to music in focusing their mind. For others, listening to the sounds worked like fast-acting sleeping pills. And some donated their own recordings of sounds as they would books to a library. Three months into the program, people began calling Musica the Musical Instrument Library, a name that didn't make sense but that I liked.

To this day, I'm not sure if making the Musical Instrument Sound Jukebox was a good idea. I've just let everything happen and flow, and it's led me to where I am now. Musica has less space and more people than before. There's also more work to be done because of people checking out the sounds of instruments. It doesn't have many more customers buying instruments, of course. What's clear is that I prefer the Musica bustling with people to the old Musica.

One thing concerned me. How would the mustached boss take this change? I can imagine him tossing out a few jokes before saying, "You've started something really interesting. Could you keep running the shop for me?" or "Do you think it's right for Musica to be bustling with people?" In our occasional conversations on the phone, I've never said a word about the Musical Instrument Library. It was difficult to explain. As of today, it's been open for six months. And in a few hours, the mustached boss will come back to Musica.

Glass Shield

Sitting in the subway, we untangled skeins of yarn. It's a piece of cake. All it takes is to hold one end of the yarn and untie one knot after another. A knot will come undone effortlessly once you spot it and pass the end of yarn through it. Holding one skein each, we concentrated on our fingers moving to the rhythm of the rattling subway train.

Our work was going well, uninterrupted, because our car was deserted except for a few passengers eyeing us suspiciously. But there was nothing to be suspicious about. Yarn can't bomb or set fire to the train. Nor can it kill. Yarn is just yarn. If anything, they should give us support, doing the wave or something, not give us disapproving looks for our efforts to untangle the skeins. We placed the untangled strands of yarn on the seats along the wall, widening the space between us as we produced more of the untangled strands of yarn. Mountains of blue and red yarn grew on the green seats.

"Look, it's so easy. Why couldn't we do it before?" said M, holding the blue skein now down to half its size.

"Don't you understand? We have a knack for botching things up in the moment of truth," I said weakly, untangling the red skein.

Two hours earlier, M and I had our thirty-first job interview. Again, it ended in the interviewer telling us, "That's enough. Please leave."

"Maybe you should've included that in your resume. SKILLS: BOTCHING THINGS UP IN THE MOMENT OF TRUTH. Who knows? It could've aroused the interviewer's pity and prompted him to offer you the job."

"Maybe you should've included this in yours: HOBBY: SNEERING AT FRIENDS OF MINE."

This was the conversation we had with our eyes fixed on the skeins. What a lousy morning. What losers. We zipped our lips and reimmersed ourselves in untangling the skeins.

"Are we on the Circle Line?"

"I think so."

"That explains why I'm dizzy."

"The Circle Line has nothing to do with it. You're dizzy because you've been staring at the skein too long. Let's take a break."

We took our eyes off the skeins to look out the window to a ground view that'd suddenly appeared. The subway train had rattled above ground, as if having timed it for the moment we took our eyes off the skeins. Under the bright light, low buildings and countless signboards flashed past us like a piece of collage art. It looked more like a series of pieced-together pictures than a view. We were looking out the window, expecting the train to go back underground. The power lines pulled taut were guiding the train along, which was still above the ground. As I was sitting in the back of the train, with my face almost pressed against the window, I could see the side of the train running on the curved rails. We were on the Circle Line after all. Two stops later, the view outside the window disappeared as the train leaned forward. The window had turned into a mirror, showing our own reflections instead of views. We went back to untangling the skeins.

My face blushed with embarrassment at the thought of the laughing interviewers from two hours earlier. M and I'd always been together when taking job tests. Not only did we wish to work for the same company, we were too inseparable to be able to imagine ourselves being apart when taking tests. We were like the head and the tail of a coin, or the front and the back of a man. With M gone, I'd be left helpless, like an infinitely thin piece of paper that couldn't stand on its edge. With me gone, I think M would feel the same. We'd taken thirty job tests together and failed every one of them. Zero success rate. But neither of us had ever considered that maybe it was time to split and go our separate ways.

We'd done the job interviews together as well. More specifically, we'd always walked into the interview room together. Some puzzled interviewers asked us if we were gay partners and others clarified that they had only one position open. We didn't care. We pleaded with the HR managers to let us be together for their interview if they wanted to see what we were really capable of. Some of them declined, but most of them approved with "As you wish."

With the ambitious goal of "rewriting the history of job interviews," we presented ourselves in a brand new style, only to face the cold reaction of the interviewers. Even though we tried to appeal to the interviewers like a comedy duo with a new gag would to an audience, we were often kicked out before our time was even up. I didn't know why. Once I asked the HR manager, as he was kicking us out, why he'd failed us. He looked back and forth at us and said, "I believe you guys have a better chance in comedy contests," before shoving us out the door. "At least they found us funny," M said, smiling.

For the interview at an online business, we did stand-up comedy—the interviewers wouldn't even crack a smile, let alone laugh. For an interview at an animation studio, we played a magic trick that turned out to be a disaster—M's prop scarf accidently caught fire and activated the sprinkler on the ceiling.

Interviewing for sales rep positions with a publisher specializing in English language instruction, we played subway vendors and got our best response. We played vendors advertising books for learning English in broken English. The play proved to be so hilarious that one of the interviewers fell out of his chair, laughing his head off. "Sorry, but we can't hire you," the HR manager told us, "because we don't make those inferior books selling in the subway." Apparently, we'd forgotten about the number one rule in preparing for job interviews: know your potential employers. We'd worked so hard to get into the company that we hadn't realized it was a publisher only of "superior" books.

Our interview preparation meeting yesterday couldn't have been more rigorous. Over dinner, we studied the information on the company's homepage over and over again. Our potential employer was a computer game company, looking for game developers and game testers. The qualifications read: basic programming skills; full of new ideas; vivid imagination; an ability to play any game; an ability to play any game as long as it needs to be played. We had none of the qualifications but decided to apply anyway, excited by the idea of getting paid to play computer games every day.

"I'd say at least we've got some imagination, wouldn't you?" M said.

"Sure," I said. "We've got a number of new ideas, too . . ." Unsure if our definition of imagination was close to our potential employer's, we still felt that as far as our aptitude was concerned, we'd have the best chance with this company of all the others we'd tried.

"So, how are we supposed to demonstrate our imagination? Play another magic trick?"

"No, I don't want to risk another fire. Let's surprise them with something completely unexpected, something totally unrelated to imagination. That'd appeal more to the interviewers. Set us apart from the other guys."

"How?"

"Name some qualities that young job seekers lack."

"We've covered that. Endurance and loyalty."

"Exactly. Endurance. That's what we'll show them. Endurance is the most important quality in testing computer games."

"How are we supposed to do that? Stand on hot stones and persevere for ten minutes or something like that?"

This was how our demonstration of untangling the skeins of yarn in front of the interviewers started. We decided that we didn't even need to practice. Practice alone is not enough to untangle the skeins. It takes perseverance and endurance. We only prepared a short speech before going to bed early.

"Instead of a self-introduction, let us give you a demonstration. We think that testing computer games is like untangling skeins of yarn. We'll show you that given perseverance and patience, we could eventually unravel all the knots."

I found that speech impressive myself! The interviewers seemed impressed, too. A faint cheer went up from them when we produced the skeins of blue and red yarn from a paper bag. Except that there was a problem. While waiting our turn in the waiting room, we'd tangled the skeins too much. Worse, the skeins we'd bought were too big. In less than a minute, we began sweating in frustration. Three minutes in, we were still making no progress. Five minutes in, we were soaked in sweat. In those five minutes, we couldn't unwind the skeins more than a foot, as our sweating palms weren't helping but aggravating the situation. M started yanking the strand of yarn instead of unraveling the knots. That's when I let out a sigh of frustration. M cursed under his breath. That was the end of it.

"That's enough. Stop. I like your idea, but neither of you

seems to have enough patience. Why don't you do some more practice before you try again?"

There was laughter among the interviewers. I fought the urge to throw the skein at them, knowing that they'd done nothing wrong. As we walked out the door, soaked with sweat, one of the applicants waiting for their turn asked, "What've they done to make you sweat like that?" I fought the urge to punch him in the face, knowing that he'd done nothing wrong either. It was our fault.

"If you hadn't sighed . . ."

"Are you blaming me?"

"No, I mean I would've done it first."

"If you'd sighed first, it would've been me who cursed."

We may have had a zero success rate at job interviews, but we had our friendship. We got on the subway feeling sweaty and hot. As our bodies cooled down in the air-conditioned train, we decided to try untangling the skeins completely.

In thirty minutes we succeeded, having produced mountains of untangled red and blue yarn spread zigzag style on the green seats of the subway train. It was a breathtaking sight, like a painter's work or a landscape in my mind. I found it beautiful.

"Quite a length, isn't it?"

"About fifty meters? No, I'd say at least one hundred meters. Or longer, maybe?"

"Let's find out. One subway car is twenty meters long, so if we walked back and forth from one end to the other with the strand of yarn in our hand, we could figure out its total length."

"How do you know the car is twenty meters long?"

"It's written over there, you fool." I pointed at the sign over the door with information about the length and width of the car and its number; information I'd study, and sometimes even try to memorize, when I was alone in the subway, so I'd have the pleasure of knowing if and when I get on the same car of the same train twice. People may go to work at the same hour by the same subway every day, but I wondered if any of them ever bothered to check out their car number.

There were only four passengers in our car. Hopefully, none of them would notice, or care, when we started walking back and forth along the length of the car with the strands of yarn trailing us. M stood up from his seat, holding the end of the blue yarn. He began to take a stroll, clutching the strand, as if walking an invisible dog leashed to it. The yarn on the seats began to trail M, twisting its body like a snake. Once he reached one end of the car, M folded the yarn, turned, and started walking in the opposite direction. As the yarn was loose, it kept trailing M. This was no way to measure the exact length of the yarn.

"The yarn keeps trailing me. Could you go over to that end of the car and hold it for me?"

"That won't work, unless you plan to hire someone to hold it at the other end. Change of plans. Just keep going all the way to the end of the train."

"Great idea. Why didn't you tell me before?"

Holding the end of the yarn, M resumed walking. To my relief, he managed to pass through the vestibules without getting the yarn caught in the doors. The gaps of the doors turned out to be wide enough for a few strands of yarn to pass through. M staggered forward to the rhythm of the rattling train. I used both hands to release the yarn a bit at a time, to keep it from getting entangled. I felt as though I were flying a kite. M was already out of my sight, but I could feel him walking into the distance. The blue yarn kept trailing M for about five minutes before it reached its end. I wrapped the end of the yarn around my right index finger in an effort not to lose it. "Does M realize that the yarn has reached its end?" I wondered, and just then the yarn pulled tight, threatening to snap. I could feel his strength on the other end. The yarn fell back to the ground.

A few minutes later, M returned, emerging through the sliding door with a triumphant smile on his face.

"This is so much fun, I'm telling you. Walking with the yarn gets all the attention. You should try it, too. Watch how the way people look at you changes. It's hilarious."

"Did you measure the length right? How many cars have you covered?"

"I don't know. Lost track once I started getting all the attention. This isn't about measuring the length. If you're not trying, I'm going back. What do you say?"

M picked up the red yarn before I had the time to answer. I didn't see any fun in it, but if this was going to be as exciting as he'd apparently found it to be, I couldn't afford not to try. I took the yarn from M. He let me, disappointed but obliging. As I stood up from my seat with the red yarn in my hand, a Metro officer walked into the car through the doors of the vestibule.

"Does this yarn belong to you, sir?" The Metro officer was holding the skein of the blue yarn in his hand. The yarn we spent half an hour unwinding had been restored to its original state in minutes. I was holding one end of the red yarn, and there was a big pile of it on the seats. There was no denying it was our yarn.

"Yes, it does."

"I've received a complaint from a passenger. He's informed me that a suspicious man in a suit was planting a bomb."

"A bomb?" My voice came out louder than I'd intended. Apparently, someone had mistaken the blue yarn for the fuse of an explosive. Who knows? Colorful fuses may be in use in some corners of the world.

"What was your purpose in laying this yarn on the floor? It was to plant a bomb, wasn't it?"

"Okay, officer. We planted a bomb, and we confess. Is that what you expect bombers to say? And it's going to blow up. Any time now . . ." M butted in from his seat. The Metro officer looked back and forth at us. Two men in suits with piles of blue and red yarn. You don't see that every day. M couldn't stop smiling.

"You guys will have to come with me." The Metro officer grabbed the red yarn off the seats and started going through the papers on the shelves and trawling the seats, fully aware, I'm sure, that he wasn't going to find anything even remotely like a bomb. Anyone with eyes could see that our looks and bombs don't match. Not that some people are born bombers, but we lack the "I will blow up the whole world!" look that any determined bomber must have. If anything, we have the looks of firecrackers rather than bombs. All this talk about "a bomb" had caused the passengers in our car to move to the next one over.

"Sorry, but we're working on some art," I explained quietly to the Metro officer. He turned his head to look at me, with a look that suggested he'd never heard of the word "art" before in his life. This in turn made me feel as if I'd never said the word "art" before in my life.

"What do you mean 'art'?" The Metro officer and M looked at me simultaneously.

"I mean art, you know."

"Do you call planting bombs art?"

"We've planted no bombs. He was just joking . . . Look at the yarn. It's not a fuse. It's just plain yarn. And we're just artists, doing a performance that'll give ordinary people, tired of life, an extraordinary experience."

"Are you telling me that laying yarns on the floors of a subway train is art?"

"Yes, I'd call it a kind of performance art that conveys,

through a single strand of yarn, our message of connectivity to modern people with broken hearts. The subway, after all, is the icon of the life of modern people."

While M giggled, the Metro officer listened to me carefully. He seemed unsure what to say. Maybe it was the word "art" or my extreme politeness, but the Metro officer had calmed down considerably. "I see what you mean, but you're still not supposed to do that in the subway."

"Do what?"

"Art."

"Oh, I see. Art. Got it, sir."

"This is a public place. Anything can happen here."

"Sorry, we'll look for other places. I apologize again."

"I'll confiscate your yarns. And can I see your IDs, please? I think I still need your information for recordkeeping." The Metro officer checked out our IDs before he moved to another car. We got off the subway at its next stop, a station that we'd never been to before and that could be anywhere in the city. We didn't care, as long as we were off the subway where the Metro officer might come back and say, "I've changed my mind. You have to come with me."

"Art? What a laugh! Too bad I had all the fun doing art and you didn't." M giggled again. Sure enough, I felt bad about myself for what I might've missed. I wondered how people would've reacted if I'd tried walking with the yarn trailing me. Who knows? It could've really given ordinary people tired of life an extraordinary experience, not that I was serious when I'd said it.

"Some of them were telling me I had a thread coming off my pants. Maybe I should've shown them my butt or something. Some of them were taking pictures of me. That was funny. I couldn't stop giggling."

We took a bus to our neighborhood and stopped by a pub

for beer. Our suits stank of sweat. As I drank beer, liquid-like yarn seeped throughout my body. I thought that if I closed my eyes and felt the beer I could figure out the length of my body.

We discussed our next interview, coming up in two days, with a maker of electronic kitchen scales. The more I discussed our interviews with M, and the more interviews we had, the more I was beginning to feel that we were evaluating our potential employers, not the other way around. Our guiding principle seemed to be that we should never work for a company that failed to understand our entertaining interview style. This principle would eventually bite us, but we didn't have any other choice. Once we started, we'd have to go all the way.

"How about bringing some foods we made?" suggested M, drowned in beer, his face red as though he'd swallowed the red yarn.

"Feed the interviewers terrible foods, and say, 'This proves we need a kitchen scale.' That's your idea, isn't it?"

"How did you know? You're a genius."

"How about adding some purgatives to the foods while we're at it? Fat chance they'll hire us anyway."

"What if they do, out of gratitude for helping them lose weight?"

"Then we'll have to enter a life of selling kitchen scales."

"I don't like that."

"Why'd you apply for the job, then?"

"I saw the potential for doing an entertaining interview using kitchen scales."

"It figures. At this rate, we're never going to get a job. We're already twenty-seven."

"*Still* twenty-seven. We'll be doing something in due time."

"Like what? Name anything we're good at. Anything."

What I said depressed M. We shut up and kept drinking beer. M and I took out all the money we had and put it on the table.

With each beer we ordered, we slid the amount of money for the beer to the left on the table. The money continued to move from right to left. The idea was to get drunk before the money ran out, but it didn't work. Watching the money got in the way. Time passed, but we stayed sober.

"Four more glasses to go."

"How come we aren't drunk yet?"

"Bottoms up!"

We held our beer glasses and drank them up, whereupon we started belching and getting dizzy. Finally, we were drunk. After all of the money had been moved to the left on the table, we went home.

The next day, I sobered up to find my head haloed by rings of headache, like the rings of Saturn. As they circled around it, the rings attacked my head at every point. I gathered M was in a similar condition. We ordered a bowl of *jjamppong* for delivery, and only drank the hot and spicy broth. The noodles in the shape of yarn were an annoying reminder of the interview the day before. We took the bowl out the door and lay on our backs, just staring up at the ceiling. We had nothing to say. We were supposed to prepare for the next day's interview, but neither of us was in the mood.

At around 3 p.m., I received a call on my cell phone. It was from a friend of mine who'd gotten a job about two months earlier at an online newspaper company. He was having a drink with us when he received the news from the company. He got so excited that he planted a kiss on my cheek. M talked him into staying for more drinks until 4 a.m., and, of course, picking up the bill. That night, he lost his cell phone and wallet, and hurt his chin God-knows-how. He thought that we'd done it. "You guys were jealous of me for getting a job and hit me." But would we? The company that gave him a job was well known in the online newspaper industry, but it was also well-known for giving its employees a lot of work for little pay. The next day, he took us out to a department store and bought each of us a tie, a present for good luck at our job interviews. And he bought himself a suit, a brand new cell phone, and a sheepskin wallet. "From now on," said he as he walked out of the department store, "I'm going to start the fantastic second half of my life."

"You exhausted yourself during the first half, so I think you're going to lose big in the second half. By, like, twenty points." M's sarcasm must've offended him. He stopped contacting us for a while. In my view, the second half of life doesn't begin at twenty-seven. We weren't even through the first quarter yet.

"Is M with you, by any chance?" he asked in a very low voice, as though he had something to tell me that he didn't want M to hear.

"Yes, he's lying here with me. We've drugged ourselves, trying to commit suicide together. No job, no money, permanently drunk." My voice came out hoarse, as though I were a dying person. I coughed up and swallowed the phlegm in my throat.

"I know you're kidding, except for the fact that he's with you. Could you ask him if he was on the subway yesterday?"

"Ask him yourself. I'll put him on. I don't think he's dead yet."

"You know I'm not comfortable with him. Just ask him if he was on the subway, please."

M was asleep. Or maybe he was playing possum, knowing that we were talking about him.

"He *was* on the subway. With me."

"With you? Was he walking around the subway with blue yarn in his hand?"

"How do *you* know that?"

"Oh, my God. I was right. That was M. I almost couldn't recognize him in a suit."

"So how did you know?"

"His pictures are on the Web. Here's the URL."

The URL took me to a personal blog called "Street Scenes." Sure enough, there was a picture of M, in a suit, looking down and walking toward the camera. And the blue yarn behind him was vaguely visible. It looked less like a strand of yarn than a blue line superimposed on the picture. The blog had a total of five pictures of him. In a rear shot, the blue yarn was featured in more detail.

Uploaded five hours earlier, the pictures had already generated about two hundred comments below. The comments were very diverse. *This is a man who couldn't get over his girlfriend lost to a car accident, so he drags around the thread of her clothes as a memory of her. This is a man traveling around the country with yarn. This picture is a fake, with a blue line superimposed on it.* I woke up M. The pictures got him laughing immediately. His laughter grew louder and louder as he read through the comments. By the time he reached the last one, he'd fallen to the ground. "These people are full of imagination. How did they come up with all these ideas? Did you read the last comment? *This is an office worker playing a dentist, walking to pull the yarn connected to the decayed tooth of his scared girlfriend sitting in the next car.*"

M rolled around on the floor. Although I didn't find the comments "rolling-around-on-the-floor" funny, I figured M might. After all, people had left those diverse comments about him. No wonder he was amused. It could've been me that ended up in those pictures.

"My boss is dying to get in touch with M. He thinks M is a street artist or something. What was M doing walking around with the blue yarn, anyway?" He sounded annoyed, apparently by M's laughter, which was loud enough to be heard over the phone. He'd always hated M's pranks and jokes. He often told me,

"I don't understand why you always stick with him." Each time he made that remark, it made *me* hate him more and more. I didn't like his choice of the word "understand" in that context. I don't believe that friendships are a matter of understanding. I had to fight the urge to challenge his remark every time for fear that it'd cost me a friend who had qualities I liked, like seriousness and curious eyes.

I considered telling him the epic story of our job interview involving the yarns, but thought better of it. It would belittle M too much. It would belittle me as well.

"You know what? We were actually doing art."

"What do you mean you were doing art?"

"A subway performance. The concept was to connect broken-hearted modern people with yarn."

"Since when do you guys do things like that? You guys and art don't really match."

M was sitting at the computer, typing. I thought he must be up to something silly again. I couldn't wait to find out what he was typing in the comment section below his own pictures.

"It's been a while. Only, you didn't know about it. We also did some art on a bus the other day."

"What exactly did you do on the bus?"

I pictured a bus. What can I do on a bus? On a bus, there's a driver, and there are seats, bells, straps, and . . . "We stuffed blue yarn in the back pockets of the seats."

"What in the world for?"

"To test people to see what they'd do with yarn."

"So what did they do with it?"

I tried but failed to come up with any ideas for possible activities with yarn on the bus. Covering the phone with my hand, I consulted M for ideas. Sitting at the computer, typing, M offered one: "Strangle the passenger sitting in the seat in front of you."

"They weren't very creative. Most of them just played cat's cradle with the person sitting next to them."

"I'm a little impressed that you guys are doing things like that. Anyway, let me call you again later."

I hung up and checked out M's comment on the Web, which read: "I think that this man was trying to tie up the subway with blue yarn."

"Weak."

"You think? Well, I'll have to try harder. Use more imagination."

We lay back down on the floor, thinking of ideas for activities with blue yarn, only to fall asleep. When I woke up, it was 7 p.m. and getting dark. I felt cheated out of my time. Everything was going too fast. I'd been thinking that even the first quarter wasn't over yet, but what if the second half had already begun, as my friend put it? What if we'd been sleeping in the locker room while everyone else had been busy giving their best shot out on the field?

M sprang to his feet and emptied coins from the piggy bank. He set about sorting the coins by type, with the carefulness of a croupier dealing cards. He slowly counted the coins as he stacked them into piles of ten. It didn't take very long to tally up what was left of the piggy bank that we'd been in the habit of robbing. M counted the coins a couple of times.

"How much have we got?" I asked, looking up at the ceiling, not so much to find out how much money we had left as to remind myself how miserable we were.

"Just about enough for a box of *ramyeon*."

"Go get some *ramyeon* then, before the money's gone."

M went out, having stuffed the coins in both of his pockets. Lying on my back, alone and quiet, I tried to imagine a life without M. It was a tough task, but it still needed to be accomplished.

It was time for us to declare independence and separation from each other, to escape from this sinking ship. We'd been living in a sinking ship, locked in each other's arms. I saw a parallel between our twosome life and a three-legged race. Even the most perfect and hardworking pair of three-legged race runners is slower than average runners with two legs of their own. More fun, sure, but slower. Maybe we'd been left too far behind. Maybe we should untie our ankles before it was too late. What would M think about that? Maybe he was waiting for me to suggest it first. I was weighing what to say to M when the phone rang.

"I've talked to my boss about you guys, and he's told me to do an interview. Is tomorrow okay?"

"We have a job interview tomorrow."

"Not all day though, right? Let's make it 5 p.m."

"What do you mean by doing an interview? We aren't doing any interviews."

"My boss has already come up with a headline: "Street Artists Stretching Their Imagination with Blue Yarn." No interview, I'm fired. So help me out. Please."

"I'll ask M."

"No, you won't. You don't need to when you guys are practically a married couple. Come to my office at 5 p.m. And don't forget to wear suits. They're for some pictures we'll be taking of you in the subway station near my office. Wait, you'll be in suits anyway for your job interview. Good."

As I hung up the phone, my gaze returned to the ceiling. "Street Artists Stretching Their Imagination with Blue Yarn." To hell with art! I didn't feel like doing anything, not even lifting a finger. I didn't want to do job interviews, I didn't want to get a job, I just wanted to be dragged somewhere by the hair.

"Look what I've got!"

M opened the door, yelling. He couldn't have had a more

innocent look on his face. He drew a sword from behind his back. It was a toy made of plastic, but still a fairly sophisticated piece of craftwork.

"Cool?"

"Yeah. Where did you get the money for it?"

"It makes sounds, too."

M smashed the plastic sword against the floor. It clanged, generating the sharp, metallic sounds of swords crossing. M walked around, striking the objects in the room with the plastic sword. The desk clanged, the fabric wardrobe clanged, the computer keyboard clanged, the monitor clanged. It sounded like the soundtrack to a war movie. Even I clanged as he laid his sword on me, lying on the floor.

"Where's the *ramyeon*?"

"Oh, the *ramyeon*. I forgot. That explains the extra money left over."

"What good is a sword without another one to cross with it?"

"I can get another one. There's a street vendor at the three-way intersection."

"Forget it. We're too old for sword fighting anyway. Besides, we need to keep the money for *ramyeon*."

"We're not too old."

I told M about the interview for the newspaper. He couldn't have been more excited. I was surprised, having assumed that things like interviews, other than job interviews, weren't his cup of tea. M excitedly talked about the idea of dressing ourselves in identical suits, like uniforms, but we both knew that we couldn't afford new suits.

We went out to visit the street vendor at the three-way intersection. All kinds of toys were on sale under the colorful lights—cars, trains, guns, arrows, and shields, mostly tacky stuff. I could see why M had picked a sword. We bought another plastic sword, and we also bought a shield made of clear plastic that I thought was glass. I was amusing myself with the thought of a shield that would break if dropped, a transparent shield with clear front vision but vulnerable to an enemy's attack, a shield that needed daily cleaning, until I touched it and realized that it was made of clear plastic, not glass. A shield with clear front vision sounded like a handy piece of armor to have in battle. After the sword and the shield, we were left with just enough money to buy ten bags of *ramyeon*. Although we were still one shield short for proper swordplay, we needed to keep that money for *ramyeon*.

The shield also clanged. A sword that clanged made sense, but a shield that clanged didn't. It clanged when it banged on our heads, it clanged when it banged on our fists and it clang-clanged when it banged on the sword. A funny set of play weapons.

"I feel like skipping our job interview tomorrow," said M, smashing his sword against the railings on the street.

"Why?" I asked, also smashing my sword against the railings.

"I don't like that the company is a scale maker. Do you?"

"No, not particularly."

"Let's skip it, then."

"Okay."

We walked on, still smashing our swords against the railings. People walking up and down the street stared at us, but we didn't stop smashing. With all the other noises on the street, it was hard to hear the sounds of the clanging swords.

"Let's try art and see what happens. We may have talent," M said, striking his sword against the shield I was holding. "Let's make the interview tomorrow the beginning of our life as full-time artists."

"You think doing art is easy? We don't even know what art is. I wish fooling around were art. We'd be the best in that department. Honestly I don't feel quite up to this interview. It's ridiculous that we're getting interviewed for our one-time mischief."

"It's fun."

I didn't see any fun in it. I smashed the shield in my left hand with the sword in my right hand, hitting hard but failing to make louder sounds. The sounds of our swords were muffled by the sounds of the cars and the radio playing at a nearby cosmetics shop. We went home.

The photos had generated five hundred comments already. While M was sitting at the monitor having fun reading the comments, I felt exhausted, with a lingering hangover and a gritty taste in my mouth.

The next day, we let ourselves sleep in, skipping our job interview with the scale maker. After a late lunch, we dressed up in suits and headed for the office of the online newspaper company. I dreaded getting interviewed but decided to embrace it as an interesting experience. I took a deep breath before walking into the office.

"I don't know much about art, you know. So he's going to be the one to interview you guys for me. He's an art journalist."

The interviewer my friend introduced handed us his business card, which read "Art Journalist." We were amazed that there was such a profession, but we were supposed to be artists ourselves, so we tried not to look impressed as we exchanged greetings. We headed for the subway station with the art journalist and a photographer. "The concept of today's shoot is going to be freedom, you know," the photographer informed us, as if we had any clue what free photographs might be like. We walked around inside a subway train with what the art journalist put in our hands, a blue string that was closer to rope than it was to yarn in thickness. To ensure visibility in the pictures, the photographer explained, it couldn't be thinner than that.

"This is far from freedom," M complained. "I feel like a slave attached to a rope."

I felt the same way.

"Okay, then I'll let you play with it in any way you want to," said the photographer, sighing. M took out the plastic swords and shield and showed them to the art journalist, the props that M had said might be needed for the shoot and had wasted an hour cramming into his bag.

"How about shooting us playing with these? I think that'll be fun . . ."

"What are you going to do with them?"

"Sword fighting."

"I think that'll be childish. Why don't we just stick to you walking with the strings?"

We ignored the art journalist and stood up with the swords in our hands, me with the shield and one of the swords and M with the other sword. M yelled at me. "Your pitiful shield is no match for my sword, you fool!"

"Don't be ridiculous. Your plastic sword has no chance of penetrating my glass shield. Through this shield, I can see your every move!"

We crossed our swords. They clanged, echoing throughout the subway car. Their sounds were louder than expected. The art journalist sitting on his seat looked agape at us, less amused than stunned by our infantile behavior. We continued to cross swords with all our might, as if determined to really kill each other. The photographer diligently clicked the shutter of his camera, although he wasn't exactly beaming.

Two kids who were sitting at a distance approached us. They may've found us intriguing for being in suits and engaged in sword fighting. The two kids watched our sword fighting with great interest. Two women who appeared to be their mothers approached us. Two old men, who wondered where the clanging sounds were coming from, and a young man and a young woman, who appeared to be a couple, approached us. The audience for our sword fighting grew and grew. Despite our arduous efforts to assail each other, our ridiculously slow and ineffective movements made us look like we were dancing rather than fighting. The two kids who'd first noticed us were pleading with their mothers. "I want one of those swords!" In about five minutes, we found ourselves surrounded by close to thirty people. They were all watching us, amused. The art journalist looked happier and the photographer busier with his camera. I gave M a knowing nod. M got it and dropped his sword. I took the blue rope on the seat and tied it around M, although throwing it over M's body was more like it. Just in time, the subway train made a stop. We stepped out onto the platform, leaving the swords and the shield behind in the train as presents for the kids. The art journalist and the photographer followed us out.

"It was fun, wasn't it?" M said proudly, and the art journalist laughed. We headed for a coffee shop for the interview. As soon as we were seated, the art journalist bombarded us with questions, few of which we could answer. We found them too difficult.

"Bruce Nauman expressed his concept of art by photographing his body language. I'm wondering if he's the kind of artist who's influenced your work."

"Who?"

"Bruce Nauman. He said that 'the true artist helps the world by revealing mystic truths.' What meaning do you attach to your actions as artists?"

"We think we help the world by revealing common truths."

"What do you mean by common truths?"

"I mean having fun."

This was basically how our interview went.

We made jokes as a way of answering all the questions. "How

do you deal with your economic situation?" "Economically," M answered. "Why did you choose yarn to be the object of your performance?" "It's been spun out of our failures," I answered. The art journalist, having an increasingly hard time interviewing us, was most interested in our performances at job interviews. With little else to talk about, we decided to jazz up our stories and present them as if they'd been artistic performances.

"Our favorite thing to do is to have fun in the interview room. Even though we never intended to get a job, we've done job interviews frequently, showing the interviewers our magic tricks, stand-up comedy gags, and performances with yarn. That's a lot of fun."

"What do you mean by performances with yarn?"

"While the interviewers were sitting around and watching, we tried to untangle the skeins of yarn, to see how long they could wait and see. It was, so to speak, a test of their endurance as workers."

"How'd it go?"

"They weren't very patient. Didn't even wait five minutes. How could they expect to find the right people for the job without giving them even five minutes? Judging people after just five minutes in the interview room? That's a laugh."

"Right. So that was an artistic way of expressing your contempt for inflexible, hierarchical organizations. How many times have you given performances in job interviews so far?"

"About thirty times, with different gags each time."

We excitedly recounted our job interview experiences. When it came to job interviews, we had a lot to talk about. Having started with a lie, *We never intended to get a job*, we felt convinced that we'd actually made art.

The next day, the online newspaper ran an article titled "The Metro Rascals Who Captivated Our Society of Limited Imagination," along with the photographs of us crossing swords,

M tied up with the blue rope, and the large crowd watching our sword fighting. The major part of the article was about our job interviews.

"Not bad."

"Just look what an art journalist can do. His article practically turns us into real artists."

Thanks to the online newspaper article, we'd become celebrities overnight. We were flooded with offers, including one to appear in a documentary titled *Street Artists*, an offer to teach a college class called "Thinking Outside of the Box," and requests for more interviews. We turned down all of them but one: an offer from an advertising agency to be their job interviewers. After all, job interviews were our specialty. Not that they let us make the hiring decision, of course. We were part of the panel of ten interviewers, but still excited that we'd get to interview applicants.

The night before our first day as job interviewers, we discussed our ideas. Despite suddenly going from being evaluated to evaluating others, our agenda hadn't changed. All we thought about was how we could make the interview as entertaining as possible.

"I just got a phone call. It's another request to handle their job interviews."

"Not again. At this rate, we're going to become professional job interviewers before we know it."

"Sounds great! Professional job interviewers. Let's do it."

There are lots of companies and they hire new employees all the time. There'd be plenty of business opportunities for professional job interviewers. Given more effort, we stood a good chance of becoming them.

After discussing possible ideas for the advertising agency's job interview, we decided to bring in firecrackers. We set them off in the middle of the interview. With a bang, colorful streamers rained down over the startled applicants. Equally startled was the panel of interviewers, unaware of our plan. The reactions from the job applicants ranged from screaming to breaking out in a cold sweat with a start and falling backward in their chairs. The idea of setting off firecrackers was to test how tense the applicants were. The one who gave a loud laugh when the firecrackers were set off got the highest ranking. You can't do anything well when you're tense.

"Who's next?"

"A securities firm. Any ideas?"

"Do you know anything about securities?"

"Of course not."

"Then how about making the applicants ask questions? They ask questions, and we answer. We know from our experience that it takes skill to ask good questions."

"You're right. That'll be interesting."

We enjoyed being job interviewers and we enjoyed discussing ideas for the interviews. We kept coming up with ingenious plans, as we'd always done. We set off firecrackers, as we had for the advertising agency, asked the applicant to try to make us laugh with the random item he was asked to pick out of a box of junk, and asked the applicant to improvise a cheer song for him—not forgetting, of course, to sing our own cheer songs first. Many of the interviewers found our questions and ideas amusing. It was as though we were there to entertain people rather than interview applicants. If we'd been as entertaining in our own job interviews as we were in other people's, I think we'd have gotten a job sooner.

Working as job interviewers, we felt like we were doing something meaningful for the first time in our lives. What meaning did it have, you might ask? I don't know, but I can say that at least I no longer had the feeling of being left alone in the locker room sleeping when the second half had begun. We used to be addicted to failure, but now we were inspiring other failure addicts. We were just happy that we could be a shield for someone, even if it was a shield made of plastic or glass.

We'd just completed our twentieth or twenty-first job as interviewers. It was for a web design agency that had an unusually large number of applicants. By the time we finished, we were too exhausted even to talk. We'd been getting tired of having to ask a different question every time, depending on the applicant's personality or answer, and seeing our plans not working for all applicants. We felt like we were running out of ideas. Worst of all, we were finding our job increasingly boring. I couldn't believe that we were already bored after only twenty interviews. We were sitting side by side in the back of the bus, looking out the windows.

"Phew, we thought this work would be easy, didn't we?" M said, still looking out the windows, talking to himself more than to me.

"You know what I think we should do? I think we should go back to the beginning. I don't think we're doing the right work for us," I said, also looking out the windows. We were looking at the same view.

"To the beginning . . . You mean to the days when we were looking for a job every day? We had fun in those days, sure. But I think we're better off now."

"No, I mean years before that."

"Starting over in college?"

"No, going back even further than that."

M turned his head to look at me, grinning. "Don't tell me you're suggesting we should kill ourselves and then get together again in the next life."

"No, I'm not."

"Speaking of the beginning, I wonder where it is. I think

there must've been a fork somewhere along the way that's led us to where we are."

"What was your dream?"

"My dream? Why ask me that after all these years? So childish . . ."

M turned his head back toward the windows and kept silent. I didn't think he was looking out the windows. It seemed like he was trying to recall what his dream had been. M once told me that he wanted to become a gardener, or a traveler, or the president of a zoo. I didn't know which one of them was M's dream. It's possible that none of them was.

M opened one of the windows wide. A breeze came in past M and to me. M stuck about half his head out of the open window. We remained silent. The moment I saw M's profile, it occurred to me that this might be the last time I was on a bus ride with him. During that brief conversation on the dull bus ride, M and I may've reached a turning point, some kind of a new fork in the road. I felt that he'd chosen to take the left path and I the right, and that the string that tied our ankles together had come undone before we could realize it. I turned my head to look out the back window. The power lines pulled taut were pointing to where we'd come from. I was thinking that a certain period of my life, which could be neither named nor defined exactly, was passing away.

B and I

I'm allergic to sunlight. Half an hour or longer in the sun and my body turns dazzling white. Well, that'd be cool. What really happens is that my skin burns red. While my skin burns red and develops rashes, my whole body swells up like a monster, a terrible sight to be avoided at all costs. Going on a picnic with cold white wine and sandwiches was an impossible dream. Although it might be fun to watch people's reactions, gasping at me in horror as I became a monster, I wouldn't try it because I'd feel pain once my allergy set in. My whole body hurts as my skin starts to swell up, threatening to burst.

I wasn't born allergic to sunlight. As a boy, I was fine playing in the schoolyard until I got a suntan. As a military serviceman, I was fine standing sentry under the blistering sun all day long. Basically I was a healthy child and a strong young man, never short on exposure to sunlight. It was four summers ago that I developed a sun allergy.

In the spring before that summer, I was clerking at a record shop. Although my job description was selling records online, I spent more time working at the shop, basically saying "How may I help you?" or "Have a nice day," as the case may be, helping the customers find the records they might like, helping them pay and giving them change. I was willing to work hard but hardly working because there weren't many customers to serve.

The record industry was going downhill fast like a car with no brakes—it's hit the bottom now—and there were record shops in every other building in the neighborhood, so getting a customer was like drawing blood from a stone. At any given moment, there were always more clerks in our shop than there were customers. If and when a customer walked in, the three or four clerks who were lounging around the shop would stare at him with a look that said they were ready to, if not really going to, serve him with all their heart, taking his bag, giving him a shoulder massage, serving him a refreshing beverage. No wonder they'd scare him off. Most customers would leave as soon as they arrived, after a quick walk around the shop. It's not like the music shop is a stadium marathoners run around in at the beginning of a race.

Some customers would ask us clerks to help find certain records. *I enjoyed the songs of singer A the other day, so I've been wondering if there is any other artist doing similar music.* Then all the clerks would get together for a conference. *How about B or C? Aren't they a little bit similar to A? Not really. A is from the same music family as D, not B or C. What're you talking about? E is the closest to A in groove alone. Nonsense! In groove alone, F is identical to A. To be fair, we should recommend G's music. In my opinion, H would be the best music for that customer's taste.*

We'd go on and on until we reached X, Y, and Z, by which time the customer waiting next to us felt compelled to buy. Who wouldn't, when three or four clerks were holding a serious musical debate exclusively for him? After closing the debate, I'd talk to him casually, trying not to sound like I was recommending a record. "If you like singer A, you must be familiar with the music of this artist."

"No, I've never heard of him."

"You haven't? Oh, no, how can you like A and not have listened to this album yet? That's a crime. Let me tell you about this record.

"If you like singer A, you must be familiar with the music of this artist."

"No, I've never heard of him."

"You haven't? Oh, no, how can you like A and not have listened to this album yet? That's a crime. Let me tell you about this record. It's a really great, historic, and innovative album. You can't talk about A's music without having listened to this one. We only have one copy left."

As you can see, it takes collective effort, conversations, patience, and threats just to sell a 17,000-won record, although, of course, I don't think there's any other record shop in the country that sells records this way.

The day I'd have my first encounter with B, I was babysitting the record shop alone. It was past 7 p.m. and the other clerks had already left. Sitting at the counter, I was listening to the new album of a famously psychedelic group. The music wasn't to popular taste, so much so that if another clerk was with me he'd have scolded me. "Keep playing music like this, and you'll keep losing customers." I was immersed in the music, my eyes closed, dreaming that all the CDs in the shop had jumped in the air, performing an improvised concert. When I opened my eyes, I noticed a customer in the shop. A twenty-something man in a cap, he was lounging around the pop record stand farthest away from the counter. I turned down the volume.

Short as my record shop clerking career may have been, I had an eye for suspicious customers, those who'd often steal glances at the counter, look at the back cover of a record too long, or stay in one spot for too long. He was one of them. I kept my eyes on him while sitting at the counter and pretending to be writing on some paper. My view of him was limited to his head and shoulders, but that gave me enough of a clue about what he was doing. From a close look at his shoulders, I could read his hand movements. From a steady look at his head, I could read his mental state. I could see that he was doing something with his hands, although I couldn't see what that something was. He could be removing CD case wraps or masturbating on the sly. He was doing something, anyway. Ten minutes later, he hurried toward the door. When he'd walked about ten steps out the door, I called to him. "Excuse me, sir."

He turned his head.

"Could you come over here for a minute, please?"

"What is it?"

"Can I have a quick look into your bag?"

"What for?"

"Just let me take a look."

"Do you think I stole something?"

"No, I just want to take a quick look into your bag. That's all."

I grabbed for his bag when he was off guard. He clung to the bag strap but the bag was already in my hand. I found about twenty CDs in it.

"These are all mine. I've been listening to them." His face had turned red. I pulled him by his clothes into the shop. I found plastic CD wraps, roughly removed and crumpled, hidden between the record stands that he'd been standing next to.

"How many did you steal?"

"I didn't steal any, I'm telling you. Do you have any proof that I did?"

Of course I didn't. The shop didn't have any closed-circuit TV cameras installed, nor did I actually see him steal. But I wasn't going to say, "Oh, yeah, I don't have any proof. Well, goodbye and have a nice day." As it turned out, the plastic CD wraps had been removed from a total of three CD cases. The title stickers on the plastic wraps were consistent with the three CDs in his bag, although they couldn't be the proof either.

I tried replacing the removed plastic wraps back on the three CDs. For quick removal of the plastic, he might've used a knife. If he did, he must've left scratches on the hard CD cases.

"How curious is that? Take a look. You see this scratch on the hard case here? It's right where the plastic was removed. What do you think about that?"

"I didn't steal them." His voice sounded less confident.

"Do you want me to call the police? Confess what you did, and I'll forgive you."

He said nothing. I took him to the counter. "I'll give you one of the three CDs as a free gift. Just take your pick."

He was looking down. Whether he was repenting what he'd done, or thinking of which album he should choose, I couldn't tell.

"I'm sorry," he said after a long silence. I let him go after giving him one of the CDs as a free gift, the one I'd picked out of the three. I wished I had my fellow clerks with me to discuss which album would be the best for him, but making unassisted decisions had its own charm. I rewrapped the other two CDs and replaced them in the stand. I put money equal to the cost of the CD I'd given him into the safe before I went home.

It was about a week later that I encountered B again. It was May, a very sunny day. I was sitting on the bench in the park after lunch, observing pigeons. As they walked, the pigeons kept nodding their heads, as if to say, "Right, good, yes, that's it, correct, all right." Are pigeons inherently positive creatures? I wasn't sure. In any case, there were positive rhythms about them. There was music playing from somewhere.

Although far off, I recognized him at once. Not a surprise, considering the amount of time I'd spent observing his face and shoulders before. B was doing a gig, singing and playing the electric guitar in front of an audience of ten or so. Sitting on the bench, I listened to his music carried by the wind. Some parts were clear to hear and other parts weren't. During the unclear parts, I watched him playing the guitar. Doing so seemed to make the sounds clear. His nimble left-hand fingers moved up and down the guitar neck like the tentacles of a mollusk. Watching them was good entertainment in itself. When his gig was over, a few people threw coins into his hat.

I rose from the bench and approached him as he was putting away his guitar and amp. I threw a bill into his hat. "I enjoyed your performance."

"Thank you."

He didn't recognize me.

"How'd you like that CD?"

He looked up and stared at me. A few seconds later, he remembered me, with a touch of shame on his face.

"I really apologize for the other day. I couldn't even thank you properly."

"I can see you're a good guitar player."

I offered him a cup of coffee for his gig and took him to the nearby café. B turned out to be older than I thought he was and younger than me by five years. We talked about music for an hour, rapidly naming our favorite artists from A to Z. More often than not, speaking in certain names, words, or proper nouns proves to be more effective in communication than speaking in full sentences. We just mentioned some people's names and became instant friends, like old friends who'd known each other for a decade. It happened like a nuclear fusion. In one hour, two separate men had been fused into one.

"Can you make a living doing gigs at the park?"

"Not really. I'm doing this just for fun. I work at a music shop by day and do gigs at clubs by night, though it's not like I make a good living."

"Why don't you give guitar lessons or something? Watching

play earlier, I felt like learning. My childhood dream was to become a guitarist."

"I normally don't teach, but I'll make a special exception for you. I owe you that much, anyway. Do you have a guitar?"

I did have a guitar. I used to practice playing the guitar on my own, choosing a guitar on my own, learning the chords on my own, practicing strumming on my own, and learning songs on my own. It was a time when I learned the difficulty of self-education. Being on my own wasn't right for learning, though it may be right for thinking, writing, or feeling lonely. I'd practiced playing the guitar for about three years without making any progress, without any idea if I was doing it properly. My guitar ended up establishing permanent residence in the attic, and I'd forgotten all about it. I'd take my guitar lessons at B's semi-underground studio, serving as his rehearsal room and living quarters. It was also conveniently located close to my record shop.

"You can't play this kind of guitar," was the first thing he said, to my embarrassment, when I visited his studio with my guitar dug out of the dust-filled attic. I don't deny that the guitar was old, but it wasn't junk. I paid a good sum of money for it years ago.

"Besides being old, it's an acoustic."

"What's wrong with acoustic guitars?"

"I hate them."

"Acoustic or electric, what's the difference? Both have six strings."

"You can't do rock and roll with acoustic guitars."

"I didn't say I'd do rock and roll. I just want to learn how to play the guitar."

"Do you know why Mr. Bob Dylan, an acoustic guitar player, brought an electric guitar to the 1965 Newport Folk Festival?"

"He'd gotten tired of acoustic guitars, I guess. But I'm not."

"Let me explain. The acoustic guitar is just a tool for accentuating the human voice. Its sounds are kept to a minimum so that the human voice can be heard. Mr. Bob Dylan brought an electric guitar because he didn't want his voice and words to be delivered properly. He believed that his voice should be buried in the music if it was to become an instrument. That's why he needed an electric guitar. The audience actually booed because they couldn't hear his voice, which is exactly what he intended. Music is more important than meaning. Mr. Bob Dylan created music without meaning. Do you think music needs words? I don't care if I can hear lyrics or not."

"Enough. I'll get an electric guitar."

"Am I not making any sense?"

"I don't know. I'll just get an electric guitar. That'll do, right?"

I bought myself an electric guitar at the music shop where B worked. The guitar was built for practice purposes, he explained, but it had fantastic sounds. He spent two hours playing dozens of guitars for sample sounds. His efforts to find the guitar sounds to my liking were commendable, but I told him to just recommend any guitar. As it turned out, buying a guitar was only the beginning of the shopping. There were so many additional items I needed to buy that I wondered if the term 'etc.' had originated from a beginner guitarist shopping for an electric guitar. First of all, I needed an amp. And then I needed a pick, a strong bag, a tuner, an effector, a shoulder strap, a stand for the guitar, etc., etc. I ended up spending almost my entire monthly paycheck on a guitar, etc., etc.

Twice a week, I took guitar lessons at his studio. While I wanted a royal road to the techniques of dazzling finger movements, he started with the basics. "I already know them," I protested in vain. "When you think you do," he reasoned with me, "that's when you should start over from the beginning." I was reminded of a kung fu movie from childhood. The master never teaches his pupil the martial arts. Instead, the master makes his pupil draw water, prepare meals, gather firewood, and teaches him to give a proper massage. The pupil grumbles until one day he realizes that everything he's been taught and made to do is what constitutes the basics of the martial arts. The moment this realization comes to him, he suddenly finds himself able to turn six somersaults and shoot palm blasts. That's how it is, at least in kung fu.

Whenever I looked bored, he showed me his left hand. The calluses on his fingers were rock-hard, as if capped with stony crowns. "Keep on practicing," he said. "You can't expect to be a masterful guitar player unless and until your hand becomes like mine." I was almost grateful that he hadn't made me do fingertip push-ups.

I gave him records for lesson fees. He said he felt bad about accepting them, but I'd have felt bad myself if I offered him nothing. After the guitar class, we'd have a drink while listening to the records I brought him. This ritual was an extension of the class. He could reproduce any guitar performance exactly once he listened to it on a record a few times, an ability that I found fascinating. One day, when we drank more than usual, he said, "Do you know what scares me most? I'm worried, like, what if the world comes to an end, before I become, you know, famous? Pathetic?"

"Why would the world come to an end?"

"I'm worried, like, what if the Earth disappears in a flash, without any warning."

"The Earth is doing fine. Why would it disappear?"

"But the universe, you don't know for sure, do you? You don't know what's going on out there. It's possible that the Earth could just disappear in a flash."

"Get famous before that happens, then."

"How could I? I'm just a copycat guitarist."

"Mr. Bob Dylan, whom you can never have enough respect for, also started out by copycatting Woody Guthrie, until he found his own voice. Besides, you're a songwriter too."

"Mr. Bob Dylan is a genius. My songs are crap."

"Someone told Bob Dylan, excuse me, Mr. Bob Dylan, this: 'Remember, Bob: no fear, no envy, no meanness.' That's my message for you."

I left the building of his studio once I confirmed he'd fallen asleep, drunk, and looked up at the sky. I remember the unusually blue shade of that early morning sky. "What's going on out there in the universe?" I wondered.

Two months into guitar practice, I began sensing something was wrong with my body. Strangely enough, my heart started to race whenever I grabbed the guitar. When I touched my chest, I could feel my heart beating at 130 RPM. At first, I joked about it. "My heart's gone mad. I think it thinks it's a metronome or something." But it turned out to be no laughing matter. Three days after first noticing it, my racing heart reached the point of disturbing my guitar practice. It felt as if I'd consumed a dozen cups of coffee in one sitting.

"Maybe you're sucking up electricity. Turn off the amp."

Once the amp was unplugged, my heart would be back to normal. You don't get electrocuted playing the electric guitar. The electricity that does run through guitar strings is no more a threat than static. The body of a guitar, made of wood, isn't electrified. Still, my heart was definitely feeling electricity.

"The herb doctor once told me that I had a weak heart. I can see now what he meant."

"You're done with rock and roll. How can you play music when you can't even touch an electric guitar? I think you've got a bashful heart. It gets excited in secret whenever you touch an electric guitar."

"How about if I practiced without the amp?"

"It wouldn't sound like an electric guitar."

"What should I do with this one?"

"Let me sell it for you. It's fairly new, so I think it's worth at least eighty percent of its full price. Why don't you bring your acoustic guitar instead? We'll have to use it for the lessons."

I felt miserable, heartbroken to have realized that my body was denying my mind the dream of becoming a guitarist. B told me to bring my acoustic guitar for my lessons, but I couldn't bear to go back to his studio. I hated to think of playing an acoustic guitar simply because I couldn't touch an electric one.

About one month later, my boss closed his record shop. I knew it would happen. I just didn't know it would happen so soon. One has to close a shop that has more clerks than it has customers. I understood it was a natural course of action, but it still made me sad. You can't figure out what's going on in your boss's head any more than you can figure out what's going on out in the universe.

Folding the shop wasn't easy. All the records had to be transported from the shop to another one, a task that'd take days for us clerks to complete. In the process, a rescue mission began.

"Hey, I can't let another shop have this album. It's a rare item . . . I'll buy it."

"This is the box set that I've got dibs on. I can't let it go. I just can't."

What started out as a transportation arrangement for the records was turning into a clearance sale for the clerks, including me. My shopping list grew and grew, until the total ransom would cost my entire monthly paycheck. The record shop was replaced by a café and the staff was dismissed.

After I quit the record shop, I developed my sun allergy. At first, I dismissed it as a temporary condition caused by too much hard work during the closing of the shop. It started one day while I was sitting on a bench. In half an hour, my body began to itch. Soon, my face, shoulders, and arms began to burn. In an hour, my skin turned red and developed rashes. In an hour and a half, my whole body swelled up, like the Incredible Hulk would when he became angry, except that, to my relief, my clothes were intact. The affected areas of my skin felt burning hot. My swollen body went back to normal as I sat still in the shade after buying a bottle of water at the convenience store and emptying it over my face and head.

I went to see doctors, who were puzzled by my condition and offered different diagnoses or guesses about its possible cause. Some said stress may have weakened me temporarily. Others blamed my lack of exercise or the dusty working environment to which I'd been exposed for a long time. I blamed the electric guitar. My guess was that electricity generated heat as it touched some areas of my head and heart, and then the heat grew intense as it combined with the sunlight, and then the intense heat created rashes as it exited my body. It was groundless speculation.

The shade had become a layover for me. I couldn't walk under the sun for more than twenty minutes without taking refuge in the shade. The shade was my shelter. I began to dress myself in long sleeves permanently once I found out that I could endure longer by avoiding direct exposure to sunlight.

Sun allergy is completely curable, given about two years of medical treatment in the shade, or that's what I wished to believe. As I had a living to make, I got myself a job with another company in a hurry. And B was put out of my mind for a while.

A few months later, I spotted B's face in the newspaper. The phrase "new guitarist in the spotlight" was added in front of his name. His record, released by a small label, was receiving good reviews, as the article read, and his guitar performance was original, with a new style that'd never been heard before. I smiled in spite of myself. I gave B a phone call. "I've read the newspaper."

"You have?"

"Nice photograph."

"Maybe I should emphasize my looks more."

"Why didn't you tell me about your record?"

"I've been busy, you know. What happened to your shop, by the way? Is it gone?"

"Went out of business. Too many CD thieves given free CDs. I'll let slip your secret when you become more famous. Let people know that this innocent-looking guy used to have a way with a knife."

"Okay, I'll have to bribe you. How much will do?"

"Send me a CD and you'll be forgiven."

We laughed as we hung up the phone. He'd sounded much more relaxed than before. Getting recognized is like removing one of the stones stored in your body. It takes a load off your mind, at least a few grams. I didn't know if B would succeed as a guitarist or not, but the more load he took off his mind, the closer he'd get to success.

A few months later, I'd meet B while I was around his studio for company business. When I called him on the phone, he was asleep in his studio. It was around 1 p.m., but his face looked 1 a.m. "I have night and day reversed these days."

"Famous artists make history at night."

"No, you don't understand. I can't get around during the day. Maybe it's the heat. My body keeps itching and my skin keeps developing something."

"Developing what?"

The symptoms that B described to me were similar to mine, except for body swelling. I told B about my condition.

"That's impossible. How can the electric guitar cause a sun allergy?"

"What do you think could be the cause, then?"

"It could be that I've lived in the basement too long. Or, it could be the excessive stress I was under making the record. Your condition sounds much worse than mine. How come you can get around okay?"

"I've learned a few tricks. I know how long before I start to swell up."

"In my case, I've decided to work only at night. The music shop I worked for has gone out of business anyway."

"I didn't know that making a record could be so stressful and damaging to your body. How bad was it?"

"It was driving me crazy. Once the recording session began, I'd keep making mistakes. My shoulders would get tense, my wrists would tingle, and I'd feel electricity running through the back of my neck."

"That's it. Electricity did it to you, too. Electricity gave us a sun allergy. I'm sure of it."

"Are we talking about the same kind of electricity here? Stop being foolish."

B and I had Chinese food delivered for late lunch. As I sat eating with B in the basement, I felt as if we were taking refuge in an air-raid shelter. In my imagined scenario, formidable sunlight bombs were going off outside, preventing us from going outside and leaving us with nothing to do but play the guitar, except that I couldn't play the electric one.

"Have you sold my guitar, by the way?" I asked him. I'd completely forgotten about my electric guitar.

"No, I couldn't, not with the music shop going out of business and all. I have it. I'll try selling it to friends of mine. Why? Do you want it back?"

"If the electric guitar gave me a sun allergy, it might also help it go away."

"You have a sun allergy, not amnesia. I think you'd better see a shrink. Maybe you need some serious electroshock after all."

B played a song on the guitar for me, the one he used to play for me often when he was still an obscure guitarist. The song never sounded better. Having released a record, B seemed like a different person, like he'd crossed a certain river.

"I don't understand why I couldn't have played as well in the recording studio as I just did with you in front of me. Actually, I'm not satisfied with my performance on the record. I wish I could put what I've just played on the record."

"You know what I thought during the guitar lessons? When I write or paint, I get to leave something tangible behind. It gives me this feeling that I'm making steady progress toward the completion of a piece of work. But when I play the guitar, it doesn't give me that feeling at all. Do you think making a record would give me that feeling?"

"No, making a record would only screw things up more. When I'm playing the guitar, I sometimes feel like I'm recording guitar sounds in my body, like, the sounds aren't released but stored in my fingers, like, the music is stored in the calluses on my fingertips."

"The new guitarist in the spotlight is eloquent, talking above my head."

"Do you know what the biggest change for me is after having released the record?"

"Money?"

"My record hardly sold."

"Fame?" "I don't get recognized at all, even by people I know. I only get around at night, you know."

"What is it then?"

"No fear, no envy, no meanness. That's what you told me. I think I've found peace of mind. I feel I can start playing my own music.

Getting famous may not be that important."

"Congratulations. You've grown up. So you don't mind now if the Earth disappears?"

"Well, I do. I'm finally starting to make my own music."

"Don't worry. I'll make sure that the universe sticks around until you finish your music."

Running from shade to shade, I returned to my office. The journey felt like crossing a large river, with stepping-stones along the way. A few months later, my employer went out of business again. Nothing feels as terrible as watching a company going out of business. Nothing feels as frustrating as working at a company going out of business. "Should I look for another job?" "No, I have loyalty to keep." "Forget loyalty. Don't stick around a campfire when it's gone out or you'll catch a cold." "But I still want to wait and see something come to completion." "Completion? Destruction is more like it!" All day long, my split ego struggled with itself.

I ended up staying with my employer until the last moment. I felt like an agent specializing in cleaning up after failed businesses as I began clearing up the office, selling the tables, cabinets, and computers at bargain prices at the flea market, trawling the office for anything useful left, and boxing up personal items. I salvaged something from the wreck: a digital camcorder. It was my prize from the "Office Clearance Event" where the employees were given the chance to win useful items.

I considered selling it at the flea market, but thought better of it. Secondhand camcorders were dirt-cheap. The whole camcorder might be worth less than its disassembled parts sold for scrap. I needed money, but it would've pained me to sell it for nearly nothing. I decided to keep it, not as an investment, of course, knowing that the already worthless piece of junk would only go down in value with time, but to make use of it.

I thought I could use it to make videos for weddings or babies' first birthday parties, but obviously I'd be no match for professionals. For a while, I wouldn't go anywhere without taking the camcorder with me, so I could be ready to shoot exclusive footage in case I happened to find myself at the scene of a terrorist attack or a car accident. Except that I'd always find myself in uneventful and peaceful surroundings. Maybe that's what you get when you always run from shade to shade.

I decided to use the camcorder on B. I'd film B's life in every detail and edit it into a documentary, which would win big at a film festival, and then . . . then what? I had no idea. But I was going to try filming anyway. It might prove to be an important film if B achieved huge success as a guitarist. B being a nocturnal creature, his documentary would have an ever-present dark shade about it, like a gloomy film noir. A nice match for his music, too. I decided to focus on making B's documentary for a while, working freelance without getting a regular job.

I started by filming his performance, and repurposed my bag into a fixed camcorder case with a small round hole in the front. The camcorder was remote-controlled. My idea was to use a hidden camera, at least in filming his performances.

For every day of the coming week, I'd visit his studio. Having struck a record deal with a major label, B was busy practicing his songs, creating ideal conditions for surreptitiously filming him. It allowed me to follow a regular schedule of coming to work, as it were, at around 10 p.m. and leaving at 4 a.m. My work involved installing the equipment while he was gone to the bathroom and changing the angles while he was gone having a glass of water.

"Have you stopped learning how to play the guitar? Bring your acoustic guitar. I'd feel better if you let me teach you instead of sitting there and listening to me play all day every day."

"You mentioned that you play better in my presence. So here

I am, sacrificing my time for you. Just worry about practicing, not me."

"You know what? I've been thinking your heart problem may have been caused by your cheap guitar. Try mine. I think I heard something about cheap guitars getting electrified."

I tried B's guitar. It made softer and clearer sounds than mine had. In three days of playing B's guitar, my heart started to race again, but much less than before. This time, it felt as if I'd consumed about three cups of coffee. I could almost say that my heart was simply leaping from the joy of playing the electric guitar. The better the guitar, the less harmful it seemed to be to the heart.

B's documentary was never finished. Practically speaking, it wasn't even started, as I was offered a job about two weeks into location work at B's studio. It was an irresistible offer with interesting work and good pay. I'd have been crazy not to accept it. As finishing B's documentary was not my lifetime mission or anything, I accepted the job offer immediately. So I began working again, then quit again, started working on something, and then quit again. My quitting was forced by my employer's situation more often than it was voluntary. Is my destiny of my own making? I can't answer yes when I walk out of a failed company. Perhaps life is a game where choice doesn't count, like a ladder game where, once it starts, the players are destined to stay on course and arrive at their respective destinations predetermined by the rules. I could only hope that there'd be no "Sorry, try again" sign at my destination. This train of thought makes me review all the choices I've made. Which one could've caused me to develop a sun allergy? How come my employers always go out of business? Why have I lost enthusiasm for playing the guitar? Why? Why? Why? But I can't remember. Memory isn't subject to the laws of gravity, so most of it floats away.

Only the part that you hold tight remains, albeit in small bits and pieces. Meanwhile, B had become a famous guitarist. Although his album sales were low, as the record industry had hit the bottom, he was now a guitarist who was often talked about by the public. With the same nimble hands that used to remove CD wraps, he now gave guitar performances that electrified audiences. Whenever he released a new album, B would send me a copy, but I'd get tired of it and stop listening after a few times through. Then I'd watch his old video clip. That raw footage always brings back my memories of him from a very long time ago. The proud knowledge that I'm the only one in the universe with access to that video may add to its charm. Although I didn't mean to make it secret, B never found out about it.

One day, while watching the video, I caught myself rubbing my left thumb against the tips of the other fingers on my left hand. It turned out to be a habit of mine that manifested whenever I watched his guitar performance on-screen. As a mother would stroke the back of her child, I was rubbing my soft fingertips. I wouldn't stop the rubbing even after becoming conscious of it. I have no idea how I got into this habit. Was it a subconscious expression of my admiration for the marble-like calluses on his fingers? Or was it a manifestation of my shame about my callus-free fingers? As I continued to watch the video, I noticed that it'd captured him saying something that I didn't remember he'd said.

"If you like something, you should give it at least a few tries. If you keep trying, it becomes really good before you know it."

I suppose I'd asked him a question, although my voice was hardly audible. Maybe I was on the far side of the studio. As B finished saying that, the videotape stopped playing. That was the end of the footage. What he said next, I can't remember at all. He may've been talking about the guitar, the strategies of playing a computer game, or a girlfriend. Any of those topics would've fit in the context. He said it would become really good, whatever that "it" may have been. Did he mean that it would improve or that I'd like it? I don't remember. I doubt he does either.

A month ago, I bought myself an electric guitar. I'd felt like learning how to play the guitar again. I convinced myself that he was talking about the guitar when he said, "If you like something, you should give it at least a few tries." I supposed that if I kept playing the guitar, I'd fall in love with it before I knew it. My new guitar is better than the old one I had, and my heart isn't showing any signs of breakdown yet. Perhaps the guitar could make my sun allergy go away without a trace, just as I'd thought it might. My fingertips are still too soft.

Runaway Bus - Remix, The Beautiful Mother of Paengdeok

My family used to keep what they'd called the "Big Book" since the old days. A thick and battered book wrapped in a blue fabric cover, the Big Book was about a span longer than B4-size paper and as thick as an encyclopedia. Initially, the Big Book was used as a ledger. Mother, who opened a mom-and-pop store when I was thirteen, started keeping the charge account in the Big Book in the belief that doing so would help her business thrive. By the time I entered middle school, however, Mother had handed the Big Book over to me on the grounds that it was "too big and thick for a ledger." I still don't know if she gave me the Big Book because it wasn't really fit to be a ledger or because she was sorry for not offering me any other presents for my entrance to middle school. In any case, I was overjoyed at receiving it.

I'd been eyeing the Big Book for quite some time. While Mother was out of her store, I'd take a long time stroking the Big Book. I liked the way it was wrapped in a blue fabric cover, and the antique feeling of a used book. Above all else, I desired the Big Book for the texture of its pages. Touching the pages felt like touching the rugged surface of a remote planet in the universe,

* This story borrows its first two and last two sentences from *The Beautiful Mother of Paengdeok*, a short story by Kim So-jin.

or the soft, green surface of turf, or the hairy skin of an animal. I'd caress the pages of the Big Book as I would the face of a girl I loved.

Once the Big Book came into my possession, I kept a diary there. I wanted to make the Big Book a diary of my own by removing all of Mother's used pages. But as the Big Book, with thirty or forty pages missing, would no longer be the nice, thick book it was, I decided instead to start using the blank pages in the back. From the way it was bound like a classic book, vertical writing in the back pages seemed more befitting to the Big Book. While keeping my diary, with the Big Book spread open on the floor, I'd feel elated by the illusion that I was a great writer from ancient times.

My love for the Big Book was short-lived. Although I kept a diary every day in the first month or so, the time between entries gradually grew longer and longer. By summer vacation of my freshman year, I hardly opened the Big Book anymore, much less kept a diary in it. To a middle school boy, there were too many things that mattered more than a diary. The Big Book was neatly placed in the bookshelf on my desk, but more as a decoration than a ledger or a diary.

Until my high school graduation, I'd still flip the Big Book open once in a while. When I needed a break from studying for exams or a piece of paper to scribble nice lines that I'd come up with, I'd take the Big Book out of the bookshelf. More than once, I tore a page out of the Big Book to write a special love letter to my girlfriend. Whenever I opened the Big Book, my eyes would automatically scan the first pages for Mother's charge account entries. Written over a few pages were customer names that were more like cryptic codes: Sesame & Salt's; Mr. Lee the Widower; the Young Wife of the House with a Persimmon Tree; Mr. Hong of the House at the End of the Narrow Alley; Curly,

Perm Hair, and so on. Written under the names were the items they'd charged to their accounts that also looked more like codes: Two Pet Bottles of Coola; Two Hatai; One Box of Coppee; Three Pieces of Full Moon Bread, and so on. These mystery items were written along with their prices in poor handwriting. Some of the items had been crossed out in red, probably indicating that they'd been paid off.

When I babysat the store for Mother, which I did more often in middle school than in my high school days, I had the most trouble figuring out how to keep the charge account in her new ledger, a thin and light notebook that replaced the Big Book once it was given to me. In the chaos of names written in the ledger, no order was found; not alphabetical order, not an ordering of the customers from nearest to farthest from the store. Judging from some of the names with no purchased items listed below them, the customer names weren't written in the order of their visits either. It was a mystery to me why they were listed in her ledger if they'd never charged to their accounts.

When a buying customer told me, "Charge to my account, will you?" I'd ask her, "Under which name are you registered, ma'am?" But she'd also have a hard time locating her own name in the book. Some would give up after flipping through the pages and say, "Just forget it then. I'll tell your mother later." Others would pull out a piece of paper, write down their name and purchase, and hand it to me. Out of a sense of responsibility to Mother's store, I'd make a detailed mental note of the customers and describe them to Mother when she got back. Then she and I'd have to go through the ritual of putting the pieces together to figure out who they were.

"Rather short?"

"Yes, she had a slender face and a snub nose."

"With a high-pitched voice?"

"Not sure. But she called me darling."

"That's Hilltop, then. Didn't know her full name was Choi Ok-bun."

Our guesswork was never verified. I simply did my job and Mother would take care of the rest. My business of flipping through the Big Book came to an end as I left for college in a different city upon graduation from high school. I briefly considered taking the Big Book with me to my room near the campus, until I realized that it'd be too big for such a cubbyhole. Whenever I caught myself missing the Big Book while reading or working on a report lying on my stomach in my college room, I found myself shaking my head, thinking, "If I brought the Big Book here and spread it open, it would probably take up half the floor." I could picture the Big Book covering my room. That's how big the Big Book felt to me in my mind, although my room was certainly larger than twice the B4 size.

It was in my senior year of college that Mother went missing. I was working on my graduation thesis in my room, with all sorts of references strewn all over the floor, when Father gave me a call. His message was simple: "Your mother's gone missing, so get down here as soon as possible." I complied, suppressing the desire to question him further because asking questions required peace of mind, which I didn't have, and would prolong the phone conversation with Father, which I didn't want. I left my room after spending ten minutes cleaning up the pieces of paper littered on the floor.

On the train home, I convinced myself that Mother had gone missing because of Father. He'd been the root cause of every tragedy that'd ever befallen her. I reasoned that since the poverty that'd forced Mother to open the store, the mild limp on her left leg, and her illiteracy could be all blamed on Father, her disappearance might also be his fault. For two hours on the train, constantly thought about my parents, building up my resentment against Father. By the time I got off, it'd reached the boiling point. At this rate, it'd reach the point where I'd punch Father in the face as soon as I saw him at home.

I still can't forget the depressing air that I felt upon entering the house through the side door of the closed store. The air was so dense, as if a huge steel plate was pressing down upon the house. Too cramped for me to breathe. No room for me to get in. I smoked a cigarette in the yard.

"You're home. Come on inside," said my elder sister from behind my back. I put out the cigarette.

"Pretty shaken up, aren't you?"

My sister and I stared down the hill at the bus terminal. I hated every bit of our cramped house, but not the part that looked over the hill. When I watched the bus terminal down the hill, I couldn't feel time passing. The sight of a bus arriving and another one departing hypnotized me. "Okay," said a voice to me, "don't think but just watch closely how the buses move down there, and you'll find the answer." Indeed, as I was observing the buses with my arms resting on the short fence, I felt as if someone was whispering some answers to me.

"Where could she be now?" my sister murmured, with her eyes still fixed on the bus terminal.

"What happened? When did she go missing?" I asked, my eyes still fixed on the bus terminal.

"Father said she'd left in the morning of the day before yesterday for a visit somewhere. She hasn't been back or called since. I hope she's not gotten into an accident or something. I'm worried."

"Did you call the police?"

"I did. They say there's no reported accident yet. I filed a missing person report. A police officer has just been to the house and asked me a few questions. She's safe, isn't she? Tell me she is."

My sister turned to look at me, but I didn't take my eyes off of the bus terminal. I had nothing to say to her. I was closely examining the directions in which the buses were moving and the intervals at which they were parked, as if looking for the answer in the bus terminal.

"How've you been doing, by the way?" asked my sister, "Graduating soon? Looking for a job?"

"Heck, what's the point of graduating anyway? How've *you* been doing?"

"Same old, same old. You know how housewives are."

The door opened and Father emerged from the room. I thought I'd feel like punching him in the face when I met him, but seeing his face didn't stir any emotion.

"You're home. I'm off to the police station," said Father in a weak voice. He seemed to be blaming himself for Mother's disappearance. I was pleased with his weak voice, thinking that it indicated his suffering and that he deserved it. Mother might have plotted her own disappearance to make Father suffer. If that's the case, she was too cruel to my sister and me. My sister went into the room, and I lit another cigarette.

Not until that evening did I notice that the Big Book was missing. I couldn't believe that I hadn't noticed that such a large book had disappeared. Only then did I feel as if my room had lost a large portion of itself, exuding emptiness and lifelessness. My room at home, only slightly larger than my college room, had never felt emptier. Now that I knew the Big Book was gone, the world seemed like a different place.

"Did you remove the Big Book from my bookshelf, by any chance?" I asked my sister.

"The Big Book? I haven't seen that thing in a decade at least, I think."

"Father did it, then."

"How should I know?"

In vain I combed my room, the main bedroom, and the store for the Big Book. All I found instead were long-forgotten photographs and a 1,000-won bill on the floor. I was as desperate to find the Big Book as I was to find Mother, if not more, as though finding the Big Book would be the ultimate solution. As though Mother had gotten stuck between its pages.

Father didn't come home until 10 p.m. He looked much older than he'd been a few hours before, looking as if he'd just passed through a magic maze where time passed three times faster. I was pleased. If aging so quickly was his way of paying back what he owed Mother, so be it.

"They say they have nothing yet. Let's just wait and see for now," said Father, taking off his shoes.

"Father, have you seen the Big Book?"

"I thought you own the Big Book now."

"I know. Did you take it, by any chance?"

"I haven't touched it."

Could it be that I'd taken the Big Book to my college room, given it to someone, or stashed it somewhere, without knowing it? But in my memory the Big Book had always been placed on the bookshelf. The only logical conclusion I could come to was that Mother had taken it.

"I think Mother's taken the Big Book with her," I said.

"Why would she do that?" said my sister as she sat up from the floor.

"I don't know. I've looked everywhere but still haven't found the Big Book."

"You may've misplaced it. Why would Mom take it with her? It's such a heavy thing."

"But there's no one else in the world who'd touch the Big Book," I said to her, my eyes continuing to search for it.

I was hoping that the Big Book's disappearance and Mother's disappearance weren't connected. If they were, that couldn't be good.

"What's in the Big Book, anyway?" my sister asked.

"Mother's charge account entries, and my diary entries, things like that."

"Are you saying Mother thought your diary was important enough to keep it company on her trip to wherever she went? Or she's been out tracking down the debtors for two days without coming home?"

"How should I know? All I'm saying is, Mother is missing and so is the Big Book."

"Maybe the Big Book's been missing longer than Mother. You don't live in this house, so you can't be sure when it went missing. Who knows? It may've been missing for one month, or two months even."

My sister had a point. But in my mind, these two cases of disappearance were the most closely connected pair of incidents in the world. If the Big Book had gone missing before Mother did, she'd have let me know. Mother letting the Big Book disappear without consulting me first was simply unthinkable. I thought about my last phone call with her a week earlier. We spoke of nothing out of the ordinary, nothing I could remember. It was a plain conversation that opened with "How are you?" and closed with "Goodbye," so quiet and peaceful that it might as well have been silence. Despite my efforts, no clue was found in that conversation, which was as clean as a freshly cleaned-up sandy wrestling arena, not even a single pebble lying around.

The next day, Mother's first witness showed up. According to the middle-aged woman, Mother was walking absentmindedly down the alley in the afternoon of the day she'd gone missing. The police officer carefully wrote down her statement in his notebook.

"Was she carrying the Big Book in her hand, by any chance?

It's wrapped in a blue fabric cover," I said, holding up my hands to indicate the size of the Big Book.

"The Big Book . . . ? Oh, I think I saw her carrying something under her arm. But was that a book? I can't be sure. She passed me by so fast I couldn't even say hello. It could've been a book, though. About the right size, too, I think . . ."

In between taking notes, the police officer tapped on his notebook with his ballpoint pen, a both imperious and impatient gesture. His gaze was directed at Father now. "You should remember what she was taking with her when she left. If the book is as big as it's claimed to be, it'd be hard for you not to."

"I don't . . . I was busy arranging the fruit boxes . . . I'm sorry."

Father's answer, "I'm sorry," sounded like it was addressed to all of us, like an apology to the witness, to me, to my sister, and to the police officer.

The witness' statement didn't tell us much, except that Mother had hurried down the alley carrying what might've been the Big Book under her arm. It still remained a mystery where she'd gone. The alley was connected to a slope connected to a steep downhill road leading to the main road, from which one could go anywhere, even to the edge of the world.

The Big Book, though it was discussed extensively, didn't seem to interest the police officer much, obviously because there was no evidence that linked it to Mother's disappearance. But I was more convinced than ever that Mother had taken the Big Book with her. But why? I didn't know. The police officer continued his investigation by questioning residents in a few houses at the end of the alley without results. "There's nothing I can do for now but to wait and see a little longer," the police officer said before he left.

"I'm sure there's something about the Big Book," I said.

My sister turned her head away from the TV. I was upset.

Why didn't anyone care about the Big Book? Why didn't anyone pay attention to the Big Book when there was no other lead? Take my sister, for example, whose one ear was still directed at the TV.

"I said there's something about it!" I cried, which prompted both her ears to turn toward me.

"What on earth are you talking about?"

"Mother left home because of the Big Book."

"Don't be ridiculous."

"The Big Book could tell us something. Shit, if only it were still here! How can you be so relaxed, watching TV when Mother's gone?"

"Let me know if there's anything I can do, okay? I hate myself, too, for leaving the house in a mess and just watching TV here."

I went out to the yard and lit a cigarette. Buses with bright headlights on were gliding through the dark into the terminal. They looked like animals, not buses. The interplay of light beams shooting out of the pairs of eyes was fascinating to watch. Although it was random and didn't follow any predictable patterns, it seemed to be controlled by an invisible master, something I hadn't noticed before in my extensive career observing the bus terminal. I wondered if there were other roads that my eyes couldn't see.

Closing my eyes, I pictured the Big Book, visualizing its rectangular shape in the air and opening it to its first page filled with names and numbers. I closed my eyes tighter in an effort to recall those names. They were too far away for me to read. If only I could get a little bit closer, I could read those names. Not just the names, but something hidden between the names and between the numbers that I didn't understand or had overlooked. But I couldn't get any closer. The names were blurry. With a honk, my eyes jerked open. It was a bus.

"Can I see you inside for a minute?" my sister called to me

from inside the room, sticking her head out of the open sliding door. I went inside to find the TV off and my sister holding a small notebook in her hand.

"What's that?"

"Mom's ledger."

"What about it?"

"You said the Big Book could tell us something. This one might help, then."

"I don't see how."

"It's got all the entries from the Big Book. I copied them into this notebook as Mom told me to. I can't say I remember exactly what they were, how I did the job, or if I did it properly without leaving anything out. All I remember is that I carefully copied the Big Book into this notebook all day long."

"Why didn't you tell me this before?"

"I would've if it'd crossed my mind. It would've been my second year of high school when Mom made me do it. I wasn't too happy and complained that I had my schoolwork to do, too. Anyway, I'm not sure where in the notebook to look for the entries from the Big Book."

"I'd say the first pages. I know the Big Book was used only briefly."

My sister and I examined the first pages of the ledger. All but about ten entries of names and numbers were crossed out in red.

"Let's go find these people."

"Are you serious? You really think Mom went missing tracking down the debtors?"

"Actually, yes. We've got nothing else to do anyway."

"If you say so . . ."

My sister and I left for the alley, each with a list of five potential debtors to track down. It'd been years since I last walked the alley. The texture of the walls, the tracks on the ground, the height of the lampposts, the shadows of the trees, the colors of the gates, the flow of the wind, and the pitches of sounds all came back to me. I'd thought that I had no memories of the alley. Had I ever walked down the alley with Mother? I didn't remember. "You're grown up now," I seemed to hear Mother's voice say in the dark, "grown enough to decide to collect old debts in the alley on your own for your mother."

The first one on my list was the "Young Wife of the Blue Gate." The gate was still blue but the wife wasn't young anymore. The "Young Wife of the Blue Gate" had no recollection of her debt. "Debt owed to your mother? No, I don't think I'm still carrying something like that. It was ages ago. So you're here to collect old debt for your mother?"

"No, I'm here to ask you if Mother has been here."

"I'm sorry about your mother. But if she'd been here, I would have let you know."

The second and third ones on my list of debtors were no more helpful than the first. The fourth and fifth ones had moved away. I considered tracking them down, but that'd be a reckless adventure. As it turned out, my sister's legwork was equally fruitless. No one had seen Mother.

"This is so humiliating!" said my sister. "You made me make a fool out of myself, stupid! What would they think of me collecting old debts from six or seven years ago?"

"At least we tried something."

"Oh, yeah? That must be comforting."

That night, as I paged through Mother's ledger, I found strange numbers. They were written on pages filled with numbers only and not a single person's name.

"I can't remember these," my sister said. "Sums of accounts receivable, perhaps?"

"The figures don't seem right," I pointed out. "163, 192, 913, 243, 1.

Neither added nor subtracted. There's no running total, either. Besides, how do you explain 1? If you assume that 163 is for 1,630 won, then 1 is for 10 won. Who charges a penny?"

"You're right. Why didn't I think that they were strange numbers when I copied them?"

"Because you have no brains."

"I don't?"

"You seemed to, at least when you were in high school."

"How about you? Is your head full of brains?"

"More than yours."

"So that's how you came up with the idea that Mother had left home to track down the debtors."

"Better that than no idea at all."

"I guess. I had no ideas and fell for your stupid one."

I went outside with a cigarette between my lips.

"Going to come up with another idea? Better be good this time so your cigarette won't go to waste." As my sister's voice followed me out, I slammed the door shut.

The bus terminal was lurking in the darkness, with neatly arranged rows of enormous creatures lying asleep on their stomach, breathing noiselessly. I exhaled a cloud of smoke down the hill and it dissipated all over before it could reach the bus terminal. The hill placed between our house and the bus terminal was dotted with acacias. It was an abandoned ground, which used to be my dumping ground when I was younger. The empty bottle of a drink stolen from Mother's store, countless cigarette butts, my transcripts, the torn pieces of a "Dear John" letter from my girlfriend, and everything else I'd dumped might've still been there. After all, the hill was abandoned ground. With a search of every nook and cranny of the hill, I might be able to retrieve all the stuff that I'd been eager to throw away.

Just then, I saw a bus with headlights on arriving at the bus terminal. It was the last one, the midnight bus. The moment my eyes caught the bus number, a long stream of numbers flashed through my mind. In places where the last midnight bus shone its headlights, I noticed numbers, the numbers from the Big Book: 913, 163, 243, and then 1. I put out the cigarette and went back into the room.

"Bus numbers," I said to my sister.

"What?"

"The numbers from the ledger. They're bus numbers: 913, 163, 243, and 1."

"Oh, is that right? So, what about them?"

"Mother wrote down the bus numbers in the Big Book. Isn't it strange to you?"

I opened the ledger to the back pages we hadn't checked before, and found pages of the bus numbers, written in different orders but at similar intervals. There were about four pages, or a week, between the pages of numbers. Why did Mother write down the bus numbers in her ledger once a week? What did those bus numbers mean? Why one week? What was the meaning, if any, of the order in which the bus numbers were written? Why'd she write those numbers in the Big Book? I was totally confused. Who else could answer these questions? Mother was the only one holding the key to the mystery.

I racked my brains all night, trying but failing to solve the mystery. By the next morning, my head had been occupied by a tightly linked chain of question marks. I had no choice left but to ask Father, the last person I wanted to talk to. He was up early in the morning, speaking on the phone. Either someone had called him to ask about Mother or he'd called someone to ask about Mother. As soon as Father hung up, I asked him, "Did Mother happen to go out somewhere every week?"

"I'm not sure, either. Had she gone anywhere?"

"She went out once or twice a week, though I'm not sure exactly how often, to make a delivery of donuts. I think that was the only time she ever went out. Why?"

"Delivery to where?"

"To the bus terminal down the hill. What . . . ?"

Before Father finished, I left the house, holding the ledger in my right hand. I'd have liked to run straight down the hill, taking a shortcut to the bus terminal, but the barbwire fences forced me to take a detour. As I walked quickly, my heart raced faster than necessary, accelerated by the combination of a premonition that something was about to be revealed, a fear that I might have to confront a dark secret, and self-reassurance that it could turn out to be nothing. As I headed for the bus terminal, I caught my breath. I was getting slower and slower, as if being pulled back by a great force behind me.

By the time I arrived at the bus terminal, my legs were shaking from fatigue or tension. I entered the office of the bus terminal. The office smelled of something funny, something that couldn't be from a single source. It smelled like a dozen different people had eaten different kinds of foods for lunch every day for a week without ever airing it out. If I tried, I could perhaps smell Mother's donuts too. And the base of this cocktail of smells was the smell of grease.

"How can I help you?" asked the woman sitting at the desk by the door, sounding annoyed, which, I gathered, was due to the smells. I'd be annoyed, too, if I were trapped in an office that smelled like this one. I told her why I was there and she referred me to Kang, the manager, who wasn't at his desk. I assumed that he couldn't stand the smells and had to escape from the office. I sat on the sofa, waiting for Kang to return. The smells were unbearable until I got used to them after about ten minutes.

"Here he comes."

A balding man was approaching the office. I rose from the sofa. Kang entered and talked with the woman about something, which seemed to include me. "If you're going to ask me something, why don't you follow me out? I've got business outside."

I followed Kang out of the office. With the engines running all around me, the idea of having a serious conversation outside seemed infeasible. Kang patrolled the alleys between the buses, kicking the wheels with his right foot. Leading the way, he turned his head slightly to the left. "What did you say you wanted to ask me about?"

"My mother."

"Who's your mother?"

"She's the one who makes a delivery of donuts here in this office."

"Yeah, I know who she is. Did something happen to her?"

"She went missing."

Without responding, Kang continued to walk between the buses. As he did, he talked with someone. He got on and then off the buses. He kept kicking the wheels. He scribbled something on the outdoor blackboard. He talked to someone on the phone. I trailed him the whole time, the antennas taken out from within my ears and directed toward him, to catch everything he was saying, including what he muttered to himself.

"The busiest time of the day is over now. Let's sit and talk." Kang sat on the bench in front of an unusually quiet bus stop. I sat next to him. While other bus stops were crowded, this one was completely empty.

"This bus stop won't have its first service until the afternoon. So you said that your mother has gone missing?"

I explained, talking about the witness on the day Mother had gone missing, about the Big Book, about the ledger, and about the bus numbers. Kang listened patiently, without much reaction other than occasional nods.

When talking about the ledger, I opened it to the pages of bus numbers for him to see.

"These numbers here are definitely the numbers of our buses."

I felt relieved when he confirmed my guess.

"Then do you see any meaningful patterns in the orders of the bus numbers written in here?"

He examined the ledger, taking his time comparing the bus numbers from the front pages with those from the back.

"Seems to me like just the orders of arrivals or departures. I wonder why she recorded something like this."

"Have you noticed anything strange about my mother lately?"

"Give me a minute, will you? I think you'd better ask Jung, the janitor."

Kang summoned someone. The man he called Jung turned out to be such an elderly man that he might as well have been called Old Jung. Or maybe he just looked old, having aged three times faster due to the shock from an accident, just as Father had after losing Mother. As Kang described Mother to him, Jung nodded.

"I often saw her sitting over there, sir," said Jung, pointing at the bench with the broom in his hand.

"What did she do, sitting over there?"

"She watched the buses, sir."

"Is that all she did? Did you see her do anything else, like writing something down?"

"She watched the buses and she also ate donuts, sir."

Jung struck me as a nervous, perhaps unstable man. I noticed sweat beading on his forehead under his old cap. Kang grabbed him by the wrist and demanded, "Try to remember and tell me if you've seen the donuts lady over the last couple of days."

Jung wiped his forehead with his palm, almost knocking his cap off. Then he pulled his cap down with an air of resolution.

"I think that the donuts lady got on bus number 238, sir."

"When was that?" I asked.

"I think that was three or four days ago, sir."

Jung didn't forget to use "sir" even to me, as though it was a habit ingrained in him through brutal torture.

"What do you mean 'you think'?" Kang demanded. "Not sure about the bus number?"

Jung seemed afraid of Kang. "There was no number on the bus, sir. But I still knew it was bus number 238, sir."

"How did you know it was bus number 238 when there was no number on it?" I asked, not understanding what Jung had said. Jung kept wiping sweat off his forehead. Sweating might be a sign of dishonesty, but there was no reason he'd lie.

"Are you sure about this, Mr. Jung?"

"I'm positive, sir. It was number 238, sir."

Kang dismissed Jung and mused on something. What on earth could it be? I was dying to know but couldn't ask.

"I'll tell you what. Something like this happens once in a great while," Kang said to me, with a look of resignation on his face.

"What do you mean?"

"I know you'll never believe this, but if you try working for a bus company, you'll understand. What happens is that a bus serving the same route over and over again disappears one day without a trace. We call it a 'Runaway Bus.'"

"A Runaway Bus?"

"It's not an official name, but slang."

"Somebody steals the bus?"

"Well, not exactly. You see, it doesn't matter who caused the bus to disappear. What matters is which bus disappeared."

"So is it a problem that the bus was number 238?"

"Take a close look at the bus over there. See the number 158? That's how you know which bus it is. But we don't need to look at the number. We can tell by appearance, even from a distance, which one's bus number 158 and which one's bus number 238. It's something you learn naturally if you work here long enough."

"How can you tell which bus it is without seeing its number?"

"A bus is supposed to serve the same route every day, passing the same buildings, crossing the same bridges, passing the same dirt roads, and loading the same passengers. As it repeats the same routine day after day, the bus develops a kind of 'stereotype,' which goes on to change its appearance in a certain way. People are shaped by environment. So are buses. The bus that passes a dirt road is bound to be covered in certain patterns of dirt all over its body. When it stays in such a rut for an extended period of time, the bus gets tired in its own way."

"What kind of bus was number 238?"

"It served a route that hadn't changed a bit for ten years. Buses serving routes that alter once in a while are very unlikely to become Runaway Buses. But bus number 238 must've been very tired because its route had hardly changed. It had every reason to turn into a Runaway Bus."

I watched closely from the corner of my eye for any sign that he was joking, but Kang's face looked serious. He took a cigarette out of his shirt pocket and put it between his lips. He offered me a smoke, too. The cigarette smelled strong.

"Maybe your mother was one of those people aware of the existence of Runaway Buses. They sometimes get on a Runaway Bus and disappear with it. But identifying Runaway Buses isn't easy. It requires extensive observation."

"Once they get on a Runaway Bus, where does it take them?"

"Well, how should I know? I've never been on one."

I stared at the buses lined up in the bus terminal. They were all expressionless. How was I supposed to identify Runaway Buses among them?

"I don't think there's anything I can do to help you. Why don't you just wait and see?"

"Please tell the police what you've just told me. I think it'll help."

"No way. Don't be ridiculous. Who would believe such a story? You believed it because you are desperate to find your mother. Ask anyone and he'd think you're out of your mind."

Kang was right. Back home, I couldn't say anything to anybody, not to Father, not to my sister. What could I tell them? Mother's gone in what they call a Runaway Bus? If I had, Father and my sister would've committed me to a mental hospital.

Mother has never returned. In the mean time, I've graduated from college and landed a job at a magazine publisher. My sister is still a fine housewife and Father runs the store for Mother. Mother's disappearance doesn't seem to have affected anything. While Father has continued to try to find Mother, placing a missing person ad in the newspaper, I've stopped trying altogether. "She's gone in a Runaway Bus," I'd remind myself, thinking that it might be a good thing for her. Waiting for the bus to work, I'm sometimes reminded of Mother. And I wonder if this bus is a Runaway Bus, although I'm well aware that it can't be. I've also developed the habit of observing buses carefully. I can see that they have different expressions, as Kang put it. All buses are slightly different from one another, although I'm not sure if those unique qualities could be described as expressions. Given extensive observation, I, too, could develop the ability to identify Runaway Buses.

Whenever I get on a bus, I imagine Mother sitting in the back and writing something in the Big Book, with no one else but me, not even the driver, on the bus. I imagine Mother and me sitting quietly in a bus going nowhere. Why did Mother record the bus numbers in the Big Book? I still don't know the answer. I can only guess. She may've sat on the bench in one of the bus stops in the terminal, carrying a donut left over from her delivery. Sitting on the bench, she may've looked at the buses. Eating the donut, she may've observed the buses closely. Envying the people getting on the bus, she may've watched the bus's rear. In the process, she may've learned the order in which the buses departed, said good-bye to the departing buses, and learned about the arriving buses. And back home, she may've looked down at the buses in the terminal down the hill in her free time. In the evening, she may've started writing down the numbers of the buses in the Big Book. The process would've been as effortless as writing down her name, no work at all to recall what she'd memorized. The Big Book may've been her diary. Even though the bus numbers carried no meaning, they may've been her diary entries.

Sitting in the back of the bus on the way home from work, I've sometimes asked Mother a question without thinking. "Mother, why'd you take the Runaway Bus?"

Then she answers, "You'll see."

"Do you mean I'll soon take one too?"

"No, I mean you'll find out."

"About what?"

"I don't know."

"Is everything okay with you?"

"I like what I see out of the bus windows."

"Do you still keep the Big Book safe?"

"Sure, I'm still using it. I'm writing in it religiously."

"Like bus numbers?"

"Yes, like bus numbers. Do you want to see what I've written?"

"What've you written?"

"Here, take a look."

"There's nothing in the Big Book, Mother."

"I'm sure."

Syncopation D

SYNCOPATION D FLASHED on and off the screen.

"Wait. Rewind a little bit, to the jumping crowd. Further, further . . . Stop."

The assistant editor of the DVD paused the screen. Syncopation D, frozen in the frame, looked bizarre. He was sticking up out of the crowd, his face in full exposure above the heads of other people. In the crowd cheering toward the stage, he was high up in the air, expressionless. How could he jump so high when he wasn't a seven-foot-tall giant or wearing spring jumping shoes? "Why?" the assistant editor asked me. "Someone you know?"

"Yes, an old friend of mine."

"Was he a high-jumper? Look how high he's jumped."

"No, it's a kind of optical illusion. Turn the wheel."

The assistant editor turned the jog dial from left to right and then from right to left. Confused, he turned his head from right to left and then left to right. "Oh, I see what you mean. His jumping is syncopated, isn't it? He jumps when everyone else lands. I guess he was fond of the seesaw, not the high jump."

"He's missing the rhythm."

"At such a regular interval? Not possible. It takes an extraordinary sense of rhythm to do that."

Going through the footage, the assistant editor and I found

several more scenes of Syncopation D. He was conspicuous in all of them. Sure enough, he looked like he was playing seesaw with the rest of the crowd. Watching the footage of Syncopation D's serious face, the assistant editor couldn't stop laughing. His head sticking up was bizarre enough to watch, but his rising face, grim and tight-lipped, reminded me of a weirdo character from an old comedy film. Syncopation D still had thick eyebrows, his trademark back in high school days. At a glance, they looked like two small black bars moving up and down.

"This guy's so funny. Let's use him for the intro," suggested the assistant editor. "Or on the jacket. I've even got an idea for the copy: 'Our Music Is Syncopated to Overturn the Syncopated World.'"

We looked for more of Syncopation D, but he wasn't to be found toward the end of the concert. By then, a majority of the crowd, including Syncopation D, had left. Admittedly, the concert was losing steam toward the end. There were many reasons, but above all else, the weather was too good. On a fine day, you shouldn't go and watch a band that plays dreamlike electronic music. A bleak rain or sweltering heat would've served it better. Instead, we had fresh air, clear skies, and warm sunshine. Basically, on such a fine day, you couldn't expect the audience to think, "Oh, electric guitars, what fantastic, dreamlike sounds you make! Melt my brains with your sound waves." Their brains were too healthy, soft, and dry to be hypnotized. The concert was already doomed when I'd decided to stage it on the beach.

"We're going to have this concert on the beach. Imagine you're listening to music and the sounds of the waves. It beats any powerful surround sound system. This'll open a new chapter in the culture of concerts."

When I said this in my proposal two months ago, everybody clapped their hands in agreement, although they may now want to hide their hands behind their back in embarrassment.

Nobody was to blame, not me, not the band, and not the audience. If anything, it was the concert's fault. Dreamlike rock concerts had been long dismissed as little more than old prostitutes wearing thick makeup.

"What do you say, boss? Use him on the jacket or not?"

"Go ahead. It's your call."

There was a zoomed-in image of Syncopation D on the monitor. His face, other than creases here and there, looked exactly as I remembered it. Twenty years earlier, he'd lip-synched with that same serious look.

Syncopation D and I went to the same high school, and we were in the same choir. It was a choir in name only, a group that was inherently incapable of producing a decent harmony. It was one of the school's extracurricular clubs for "special activities," as they were called, designed to help the students develop individuality, engage in healthy hobbies, learn special functions, and take part in the activities of democratic life, except that it was completely inactive until special occasions arose, special occasions being the annual school festivals in which no one took any interest. The choir and the audience couldn't have cared less about each other. When the choir made a mistake, the audience didn't care. When the audience didn't listen, the choir didn't care. When the audience threw stones at the choir, the choir didn't care. When the stones missed the choir, the audience blamed themselves. When the choir stopped after only one song, the audience understood. Indifference was the choir's motto. That's why I chose to join it in the first place. If I had to do special activities at all, I preferred ones that drew no attention. My parents had just divorced and my runaway brother was planning another escape from home. For my part, I was looking for a similar escape from life. To a high school student in that situation, the word "harmony" felt like an ideal yet improbable utopia.

The most passionate member of the choir was Syncopation D. He wasn't like most of us, who picked the choir randomly and apathetically from a list of extracurricular clubs. From day one, he was different. When the music teacher asked if any of us, by any chance, by any slim chance, would want to be the leader of the choir, his hand shot right up in the air. He looked so serious that both the music teacher and the rest of us were confounded. "Oh, okay. You're the leader, then. Your job is . . . well, there's not much to do, really, other than to make copies of the score of the song for the festival and, well, that's pretty much it. Anyway, you are the leader now . . . Congratulations." When the teacher finished congratulating him, he asked her immediately, "What are we going to sing for the festival?"

"Well, it's too early to decide, isn't it? The festival is five months away, you know. We have plenty of time left to think about it."

"What about for today's practice?"

"Practice? Oh yes, practice. Today's the first day, so why don't I just give you guys a break and let you study independently?"

"You mean we're going to practice singing individually?"

"Okay, do your work now. Your midterms are coming. If you want to practice singing, you're free to do so outside."

With no impending special occasions, we all sat in the music room and studied independently. Whether the disappointed Syncopation D went outside and practiced singing, I don't remember. No one paid attention to him. The next week and the week after that, we continued to study independently, although the music teacher had said that she'd let us do so only because it had been the first day. Sitting in the large music room, we learned English vocabulary, math formulas, or world geography by heart. Everybody knew that joining the choir meant free timeto study independently without doing any activities. Everybody but Syncopation D. I used the time to catch up on my sleep, lying face down on the music table. The choir didn't start to practice until four months later, one month before the festival.

It took us less than a minute to decide what to sing for the festival. One of us had recommended (rather, said the title of) one of the most popular ballads of the time, and the rest of us agreed. I remember nothing about that song other than that it was a bad choice for harmony. The song was so simple and easy that one had to wonder why a bunch of people would bother trying to sing it together. Once we decided on the song, we went right back to studying independently. It was a week later that our practice finally began. I still remember vividly that moment.

"It's such an easy song. Let's sing it once together and get it over with. Here we go."

We started singing to the music teacher's piano accompaniment, unaware of the presence among us of an amazingly terrible, off-the-beat, and out-of-tune singer who'd turn out to be Syncopation D. Our singing was going well until we were distracted by a kind of evil spirit felt in the song and among our voices. The evil spirit soon engulfed our voices, messing up the song in about five measures. The music teacher stopped playing the piano, infuriated. "Knowing your motives for joining this group, I don't expect to make the best choir out of you. But I still expect a choir! I've never heard worse singers."

We tried again from the beginning, but the evil spirit didn't go away. On our third try, the music teacher finally sensed that evil spirit. "Wait, where is this voice coming from? Keep singing."

The music teacher paced up and down before the twenty-two of us lined up in three rows, listening. We tensed up, thinking, "I can't be the one messing up the chorus, can I? But what if I am?" Our anxiety showed in our singing, and when anxious souls were singing, it was no longer a song.

"Leader, I think it's your voice. Let me hear you sing, you alone."

Syncopation D's singing wasn't so bad. It sounded sweet enough and right on the rhythm. The music teacher looked puzzled. There was definitely something wrong with his singing, but it wasn't possible to tell exactly where and how it went wrong, or how to fix it.

We tried singing all together again with the same result. As soon as Syncopation D's voice popped up, it led us astray, messed up the melody and sent the rhythm out of control. His voice was a highly contagious virus. The music teacher advised him to leave the choir, but Syncopation D insisted on staying. He said he'd already told many people that he'd sing in the choir for the festival.

"Fair enough. I'll let you stay on one condition. Never make a sound. Just lip-synch. Understood?"

For the life of me, I can't remember Syncopation D's real name. I can recall what the music teacher said, what Syncopation D said in response, and how the rest of us whispered to one another, but not his real name. I've never uttered his name, even though Syncopation D has been the subject of conversations that I've had with the old choir members from high school. But I've always thought that the letter D fits him well. Although I don't remember whether the letter D represents one of his initials, the D note that he was stuck on, or something else, the sight of the letter D always made me nervous, a precarious feeling that it was on the brink of collapse. In any case, we often talked about Syncopation D. He was fun to remember and discuss. And I liked the funny and pleasant feeling of pronouncing "Syncopation Dee." Once his name was brought up, the better part of our conversation was spent admiring his amazing syncopation from our first practice.

It was two weeks after the concert DVD was released that Syncopation D contacted me. I was going to refuse his call.

"Someone's on the phone for you. Says he's a friend of yours from high school. Does the name Syncopation D ring a bell?" Discomfort was my first feeling when I received that message. There were many reasons. First, he and I weren't that close. Second, I was certain that he'd called me about his photo on the DVD jacket and about the concert. Third, I had a strong feeling that he was going to ask me a favor. When you're pushing forty, the only time you call someone is when you want something from him. When you're pushing forty, such calls become more frequent. Before I could find an excuse not to answer the phone, he was put through.

"Remember me? This is Syncopation D. That's what I was called in high school, anyway."

I wasn't sure if I should say yes or no. If I said yes, he'd get down to business. If I said no, the conversation would go on longer. I'd rather have it short.

"Sure, I do remember you. Long time no see. It's been, what, twenty years? What's up? I didn't expect to hear from you."

"The concert you produced not long ago, you know. My face was on the cover of the DVD. I thought you used the photo knowing that it was me. You didn't know?"

I didn't feel like discussing the concert. I should've said no when the assistant editor had asked me if it was okay to use Syncopation D on the jacket.

"Oh, was that you? I didn't know that. I'm not on the team that makes the DVDs."

"I loved the concert so much I went to buy the DVD. And there I was. On its cover! Do you have any idea how surprised I was to find that?"

He loved the concert so much? Then why did he leave in the middle of it? I almost interrogated him but didn't, not wanting the conversation to go on longer than it already had.

"Oh, so you were. I'm sorry. I guess we were supposed to ask your permission or something before using your photo."

What are you getting at? Is that what you want? Do you want some kind of compensation? Do you want to blame me for using your photo without permission?

"Permission? No, no, I was just . . . fascinated . . . and grateful. It's an honor, really, to have my photo on the DVD of such a nice concert."

Here's what I hate about talking on the phone. It leaves me blind to the true intention of the person on the other end of the line. It takes seeing his eyes twitch or his lips quiver to tell if he's pulling a trick. I had no option but to wait until he got down to business.

"I'd like to ask you a favor. It's not a big one."

This was it. I knew this was coming. I knew it. I haven't aged for nothing after all.

"What is it?"

"Can we discuss it in person? I'd like to see you and catch up after all these years."

"I'm sorry, but it's quite hectic around here. I've got a new concert to produce, and a lot of commitments, too. Can't this be done over the phone?"

"You're busy. Yes, it can, but I just thought it'd be nice if we talked in person. Besides, I have someone I'd like to introduce you to."

"Introduce me to whom?"

"You produce a lot of concerts. So you may've heard of him. He's the leader of a group called Double Dubbing. He's preparing a concert. And I . . ."

The rest of what he said faded out. The moment I heard the name Double Dubbing, my mind halted. Double Dubbing were rising stars, acclaimed for their near perfect music, all without giving a single public performance yet. I was also a fan of Double Dubbing, especially their second album, which was on my top ten list.

"Do you know Double Dubbing?"

"Yes, I've listened to a couple of their songs. Let's get together, then, for old times' sake. When's a good time for you?"

Syncopation D may've seen through me, the fact that it was the name Double Dubbing that'd changed my mind. But I didn't mind if he did, as long as he would let me meet them.

The next day, it took me almost an hour to pick out an outfit for the appointment that evening. It shouldn't be too casual or too formal. Picking one somewhere in between with a look that said both, "I dressed up just enough to show respect for the group I barely know or like" and, "I just threw this on, but look what a nice fashion sense I have" wasn't easy. I was ten minutes later, on purpose, in arriving to our appointment. The two were already there, talking. Syncopation D introduced us to each other. "K, this is Dubbing Lee, the leader of the group Double Dubbing. Dubbing Lee, this is K, my high school buddy and an able concert producer. Dubbing Lee, you couldn't think of a better name, could you?"

"I don't see anything wrong with it. It's an easy name to say. Don't worry, Mr. Lee. I like your name," I said, laughing.

In less than five minutes, I could see that the two were close. Despite a roughly ten-year age difference between the two, Dubbing Lee and Syncopation D seemed to be in a relationship that'd already transcended age. I could tell by their eyes looking at each other. They seemed to be connected with an invisible string, which, like barbwire, denied my access. The unpleasant feeling that came over me was unavoidable. After all, I'd never met Dubbing Lee before and hadn't met Syncopation D for twenty years. It was only natural for me to feel awkward in their presence.

I decided to lead the conversation. "You know what everybody called him back in high school? He didn't tell you? Syncopation D. You were really great back then. As soon as you began singing, we'd all lose our sense of rhythm. It was amazing. We'd tease you with phrases like *The Black Hole of Rhythm* or *Looking for Lost Melody*. I hope you still have that sense of rhythm. Sometimes I miss your syncopation."

"Really? I don't believe it. As far as I know, he's a great singer."

"I know he is, except when he isn't, when he's singing with others. His melody and rhythm have no social skills. I'm worried about their social life, aren't you?" I said, laughing.

"I guess I'll have to try singing with him sometime, to see if it makes my melody and rhythm disappear, too."

"I have to warn you, though, Mr. Lee. It could turn a rising star into a falling star. So go ahead and try it if you want to end your singing career," I joked, laughing.

Syncopation D said nothing, just quietly listening to us talk without either laughing or looking offended. That was as far I could lead the conversation. I couldn't talk about twenty-year-old episodes all day.

Besides, I was conscious of Syncopation D's reaction. I couldn't go on making fun of him when he didn't laugh. Twenty years is a long time, long enough to have changed a man into a completely different one. How he'd changed, and what kind of man he'd become, I had no idea. We ate together and Syncopation D and Dubbing Lee did most of the talking, discussing topics that mostly concerned Dubbing Lee, such as concerts or new albums to be released. Occasionally, I cut in on their conversation, but found it hard to jump the string connecting their eyes.

"The favor I was going to ask of you is, can you do consulting for this concert?" Syncopation D finally raised the topic over dessert.

My guess had been proven wrong. What I thought he would ask me was: 1) Can you produce the concert for us at a discount? or, 2) Can you produce the concert for us for free? I'd even rehearsed the answer: "Okay. I wouldn't normally do this, but I will make a special exception for you, my high school buddy." A Double Dubbing project was a potential breakthrough in my career that could launch me from a B-list to an A-list concert producer. In my ten-year career of producing concerts, I hadn't done a major one yet. Not that my career had been bad, but it certainly lacked a serious accomplishment. If I pulled off a Double Dubbing project with success, many artists would start wanting me. That'd position me to start producing really wonderful concerts. These were the thoughts that I'd entertained myself with while picking out my outfit and coming to the restaurant.

"Can I do consulting? Who's going to do the producing?"

"Well, I am. I think I'll give it a shot."

There was an air of confidence in Syncopation D's voice.

"You are? You're going to produce the concert? Have you ever learned how?"

"No, not at all. I love watching concerts, but I know nothing about production. That's why I asked you to consult."

"I admire your courage, but this isn't a game. Do you know what I've learned in my ten-year career in concert production? That this is a superman's job. That a sloppy producer could screw over hardworking artists. If I were you, I'd hire a professional like me. Look around. Use your friends. That's what friends are for. It's not like I'd rip off my friend. I'd even do it for free."

"You don't understand. He's got insight."

"It takes more than insight, Mr. Lee. Otherwise, I'd have become a god in this business by now. It takes sensibility to inspire people, ears for sounds, charisma to manage the staff, marketing skills, an ability to handle accidents . . . The list goes on and on and on. These are all the basic requirements."

"You scare me. Okay, if you say so. Let me think about it more before I get back to you."

Syncopation D stepped back from the conversation, leaving me even more impatient. I couldn't understand why he wouldn't let me produce the concert. My offer of free services did little to change his mind.

The meeting with Syncopation D ended without results. On my way home, I was upset, not knowing why. I hated Syncopation D for showing up after twenty years, even though he hadn't wronged me in any other way. Back home, I drank by myself until 4 a.m. As I fell asleep, I felt the weight of being forty pressing down on me.

It was three days later that I met Syncopation D again. He came to my office. That was where I suggested we meet when he called. I was hoping that he'd change his mind after seeing me at work. In my office, I set the stage to convince Syncopation D to hire me, with my desk made a little bit messy, a stack of concert proposals placed on the floor, and the minutes of a brainstorming meeting wide open.

"Sorry about the mess, but I couldn't leave the office to meet you outside. Besides, cafés that are right for conversation are hard to find these days. Rubbish songs have taken control of cafés."

Syncopation D looked around my office. The props I'd set up caught his eye. Pushing the open book to one side on the table, I showed him to the sofa. I was an excellent actor, who knew his way around on the stage, with a perfectly good idea of how to say his lines and how to behave.

"So you studied silent film? Do you teach now?" I began. I wanted to ask him questions like, "What's your major? It's not concert production, is it? Then why do you want to do it?" When he'd said the other night that he'd studied silent film in graduate school, I thought that the subject fit him well. After all, silent film required no rhythm or melody.

"Yes, I teach a few classes, do some freelance writing, and even edit a film magazine. The sorts of jobs that don't pay much."

"Same here. For slaving away several months on a concert, I get paid little. Just enough to feed myself. I thought I'd be something when I was forty."

"But you are. I can see you're established."

"Established? Yeah, I'm established, I guess, right on this sofa. Not that getting a comfy sofa like this one is easy, but this is all I have."

I sounded like a loser. But I didn't say it to make Syncopation D take pity and let me produce the Double Dubbing's concert. I meant it.

"Do you remember the festival back in high school, when we sang in the choir?"

I never expected that Syncopation D would bring it up first, one of the greatest humiliations in his life, for all I knew. After our performance at the festival, we all dreaded the thought that Syncopation D might hang himself. He screwed up big time, although the rest of us weren't any better, having practiced little, if at all, over the weeks spent learning English vocabulary, math formulas, and the chronological tables of world history by heart. Staged in the outdoor hall with an audience of as many as fifty students and a couple of adults, our performance was going well until the end of the first verse. Though doing our best singing, we couldn't wait to get it over with. For his part, Syncopation D was also doing his best lip-synching, at least through the first verse. It wasn't until the second verse was about to begin, following the interlude, that Syncopation D's voice popped up. He'd begun singing, and syncopated at that. Instantly, it messed everything up. The choir members panicked and the music teacher, our conductor, her eyes wide, glared at Syncopation D, mouthing for him to stop. But Syncopation D kept on singing with passion, his eyes clamped shut. Those who might've otherwise been uninterested in the choir were attracted to the hall, and the audience was plenty entertained by our lousy performance, laughing louder than our singing. Infuriated, the music teacher stopped the accompaniment. The choir also stopped singing. Syncopation D didn't, his eyes still closed. The music teacher approached him and slapped his face. "You moron! Stop singing! Shut up! Shut up!" The music teacher slapped his face two more times to the rhythm of "Shut up!" before disappearing behind the stage, still outraged. There was no point in us staying on the stage any longer. We stepped down, leaving Syncopation D alone there.

"I do. How can I forget it?"

"The day after the festival, I dumped my entire collection of about three hundred CDs. I spent all day in my room removing the CDs from their plastic cases, one by one. Once I bagged them up and tossed them away, I felt so liberated. I've never shared this story with anyone else before."

"Why did you sing that day, anyway?"

"Couldn't help it. I couldn't stand myself lip-synching in front of the audience. That was so humiliating. By the time the song reached the interlude, I suddenly felt confident in myself. 'No one would notice it if I sang in a very small voice,' I thought to myself, 'so small that no one else could hear.' It would be okay if I kept it very low."

"You had no idea who you were."

"Who I was? Yes, maybe you're right. I never listened to music again until I graduated from college. Nor did I sing, of course. Once I forced my ears to shut down, I couldn't hear any music. It was amazing."

"But you still want to try concert production."

"Have you ever watched any silent film?"

"Sure, Charlie Chaplin's."

"Many of the early silent films are fascinating. Silent porn films, for example. You haven't seen one, have you? Imagine watching a couple have sex with no sound at all. Throughout the scene, you think you hear things, like groans, but they aren't real sounds. It's an auditory hallucination, so to speak. I wonder what went through the minds of people watching silent porn films back then. My favorite silent film is called *The Exhibition of Sounds,* where the camera's fixed on railway tracks, a railway track stretching out, a railway track coming to an end, a railway track making a curve, or a railway track disappearing. The images themselves are a kind of sound."

Laughing, I said, "Is this what you teach in one of your classes? It'd be interesting to watch a silent porn film."

"What I'm trying to say is, that film opened a new door for my life."

"So you went on to film railways across the country or something?"

"I started my own project in graduate school. While my classmates were working on short films, I recorded songs, the songs of people."

"Like music in concert halls?"

"No, unaccompanied songs. After watching that film several times, I suddenly felt like studying and documenting tone-deaf people."

"How were you supposed to find them? They're not exactly going around advertising themselves."

"It wasn't easy. I asked around and worked part-time in a karaoke so I could listen in. Once I found tone-deaf people, I recorded what they sang, unaccompanied. You know what's funny about them? Most of them had been aware that they were tone-deaf, whereas it had never occurred to *me* that I might be tone-deaf until the music teacher slapped my face. Not that they'd figured it out themselves. They'd just been told, brainwashed all their life. 'I'm tone-deaf, I'm tone-deaf.'"

The more I heard the story of Syncopation D, the more disturbed I felt. I wasn't sure if it was because he was telling me such an old story or because I wasn't part of the story of his life-changing experience. In any case, I didn't want to hear it. A long time had passed since the music teacher slapped Syncopation D in the face. The music teacher paid a big price for it, but the rest of us may have slapped his face, too. If that was the case, then we owed him an apology. My memory was blurry. Too much time had passed for me to feel sorry for him.

"Why do you want to do concert production?"

"In a nutshell, I'd like to prove that I'm not tone-deaf."

"What if you do? What difference does that make? Will it solve anything?"

"Well, I'll have to try it to find out."

I decided to help Syncopation D out. There were many reasons. First, I didn't want to lose him to another production company. Second, he let me handpick the staff and handle the technical aspects of the concert, like sounds, equipment, and stage settings. Third, I had absolutely nothing to lose. If the concert succeeded, I'd get my share of reputation. If it failed, I could still walk away, unscathed. It was a good deal. And it was a good opportunity for me. My inexplicable feeling of indebtedness to Syncopation D may've also had something to do with it.

Syncopation D was the executive producer, and I took on the roles of stage manager and assistant producer. Syncopation D was responsible for the artistic aspects of the concert, and I the technical aspects. But the truth was that I wasn't really responsible for the technical aspects. For any failed concert, the biggest reason lies in the concept or the story, not the technical aspects. Sound or lighting accidents do occur, but they're minor defects, easily forgotten as long as the main story appeals to the audience.

Syncopation D turned out to be a more competent producer than I thought he'd be. Though my assistance played a big role, he was quick and much more intuitive than I expected. Working on the project with Syncopation D reminded me of ten years earlier, when I started out in the concert production business as an apprentice laboring under an abusive executive producer. I was as nervous and disciplined as a soldier at war. I worked twenty hours a day, desperate to avoid making mistakes and to get recognized by the executive producer. To understand the music of the artist I was preparing a concert for, I listened to it around the clock, but never got tired of it. The more I listened, the more new ideas came to me. I thought of concert ideas even in my dreams. When I was made the assistant producer after three years, everyone was surprised, everyone but me. When I was made the producer another five years after that, everyone was surprised again, everyone but me. I knew it'd happen. Working on the project with Syncopation D felt like going back in time to my younger self as an assistant producer. My roles were the same as then, but I was no longer nervous. On the contrary, I was enjoying the work. Whether it was because I was taking on the roles of the assistant producer or because I was free of responsibility, the work felt easy to the point of making me wonder if maybe I was better as the nagging second man than as the leader.

The main theme of the concert was "When Double Dubbing Meets Silent Film." To be honest, I was a little impressed when Syncopation D presented the synopsis. It was brand-new, though not perfect, full of ingenious and interesting ideas with the potential to create something I'd never seen before, at least not during my ten-year career. For instance, adding several scenes from silent films to Double Dubbing's songs that were mixes of a variety of music was a novel idea. I liked the idea of a DJ remixing the background music of silent films into new music. The idea of the musicians performing like silent film actors and walking around on the stage to the background music of silent films sounded like fun. There was also the idea of playing a short film so that Double Dubbing could make new music that would go with the picture. Most importantly, Double Dubbing's music and the silent film were a perfect match. The two elements were in a good balance, neither one overpowering the other. The project was made possible by Syncopation D's good understanding of both silent film and Double Dubbing's music.

"I couldn't have done it without you."

Syncopation D's compliment pleased me, and it was also true. I was a competent producer, too. Knowing everything there was to know about concerts, I was fully prepared. I handled every aspect of the project more effectively and efficiently than ever. Syncopation D and I made good partners. One week before the concert, Syncopation D said, "Can I ask you one more favor?"

"Don't scare me. What could it be now?"

"I have guests I'd like to invite to the concert. Can you contact them for me?"

"Why do I have to contact *your* guests?"

"Because they're your friends, too, the old choir members from high school. It's kind of awkward for me to contact them myself. I know you're still in touch with some of them."

As a matter of fact, I was. I had my own reasons to stay in touch with several of the old choir members. But was it a good idea to invite them to the concert? Considering the humiliating experience they'd shared with Syncopation D, they might or might not want to meet him again. But this was a perfect opportunity, for me at least, to do what they'd often complained about me not doing as a concert producer: send them free tickets to a concert.

"I see. That's a good idea. A reunion of the legendary choir members after twenty years. I'll contact those I can, and they'll take care of the others. But I doubt we can bring all of them back together."

As I contacted those I could, I was updated on the news of the others. The choir at our high school had had twenty members. One of them died two years ago, killed in a car accident. I wasn't close enough to him to have been informed when it happened. Another of them was fighting cancer, liver cancer, with less than six months to live. I didn't remember his name very well. I hesitated to call him, but called anyway. He said, tearfully, that he was sure to come. The rest of them, minus one on a business trip overseas, two living in other countries, and three that couldn't be reached, said they'd come. That made thirteen of us getting together.

Talking to them on the phone, I tried but failed miserably to recall their faces from high school days. Everything from those days was a blur in my memory. There was no way I could remember their faces, not when I hardly had the time to look at them. A majority of them weren't in the same class as me. During the times when we were in the same room, we spent more time studying independently than singing together. No wonder I couldn't remember their faces. I reserved good front seats for the old choir members.

The concert was highly anticipated and sold out three days in advance. As that didn't happen every day, I even got media coverage. When a reporter from a TV network came for a brief visit and shooting of our preparations for the concert, I coaxed him into doing an interview with me.

"Singers complain that nobody buys their albums anymore.

That music is dead. But the future of music doesn't depend on selling albums. It depends on getting people to come to concerts. It's possible to listen to albums for free, but it's not possible to watch concerts for free. This is where new music should start." My message appeared on national television. I noticed in the caption "the producer of Double Dubbing's first concert" added to my name. The title wasn't exactly true, but I didn't bother asking them to correct it. Once the concert came off successfully, many artists would start wanting me. The day before the concert, I carefully checked the sound and lighting systems many times over. I was going through an important moment in my life. I felt anticipation and tension pulling my body tight.

On the day of the concert, with two hours to go before the opening, Syncopation D and I sat on the stage and had a cup of coffee. The concert was now ready, with dry rehearsal and camera rehearsal all over. The empty seats were staring at us.

"I'm nervous. This is what it feels like to give a concert. It's finally starting."

"Relax and enjoy the ride. It's going to be a historic night tonight, a new performance that no one's ever imagined."

Syncopation D and I cheered for each other before the final check. While I was busy behind the stage, one hour passed as quickly as one second. Tick-tock. And suddenly all the seats were full. From behind the stage, the hustle and bustle of the crowd sounded like waves. The crowd was soon going to turn into a tsunami and engulf the hall. I peeked between the curtains and found few empty seats in the stands. Cameras kept flashing and some fans screamed. They were nervous, too. When the lights went out, the sounds of waves in the stands died down. The concert opened with a short silent film. A man in a suit was lying on a railway track, attempting a suicide. The train didn't come. The man got up and then lay down again. The man appeared to be uncomfortable and turned in his lying position. The next day, the man showed up again, this time with a pillow in his hand. He placed the pillow on the railway track before he lay down on it. The day after that, the man showed up with a blanket. The day after that, the man showed up with a shack on his shoulder. The man placed the shack on the railway track. The shack was lit from within. The light went out and a train was seen approaching from far off. The train was getting closer and closer. When the train almost came in contact with it, the shack was lit again. The moment when everyone was expecting a collision, bam, they heard guitar sounds.

"Wow!"

With the flashing lights, Double Dubbing made an appearance, generating a kind of tsunami wave. Even to me, it was a dramatic opening, with Double Dubbing members bursting out through the screen on which, only a few seconds earlier, the black and white silent film had been projected. The train rushing toward the shack had turned into the real Double Dubbing members jumping out at the crowd. Double Dubbing's music was great, at least ten times more powerful than on their albums or in their rehearsals. Their music was mesmerizing, and it refused to be placed into a certain genre. It was more powerful than rock, freer than jazz, more elegant than classical music, and more rhythmical than funk. Double Dubbing looked so confident and competent in their performance that it was hard to believe that it was their first concert. This may've proved that Syncopation D's storyboard was well thought out.

The crowd got most excited when Double Dubbing started performing to the scenes of a silent film, a very short one titled *Sneeze*. The opening scene was a close-up shot of a woman's face. Her nose itched. She was about to have a sneezing fit. She tried to hold it back, with difficulty. That was all.

For the scene of the woman's near-sneeze moment, Double Dubbing performed funny music. The silent film's scene drew a burst of laughter from the crowd. Double Dubbing's performance caused another burst of laughter. The woman's frown was subtly off the beat with Double Dubbing's music, not exactly in rhythm but a little bit syncopated, which the crowd seemed to find more amusing. I wondered: "Could it be that Double Dubbing dedicated this music to Syncopation D? 'Syncopated Music for Syncopation D?'"

The concert was over, but the crowd stayed, shouting "encore!" An encore had been selected and rehearsed, of course. Double Dubbing reappeared on the stage, and all the lights were out. The sounds of the crowd died down in the dark. Various sounds had been flattened out into a long line. Then there was music, faint and barely audible. According to the storyboard, it was time to play their biggest hit song. Something must have gone wrong.

"Sound, what's the matter? Check the sound," I demanded.

Then Syncopation D's voice sounded through the wireless headset. "No, it's going well, following the storyboard you don't know about. This is my present to the old choir members from twenty years ago."

The faint sounds rose in a crescendo. They flew out of the speakers and seeped through the crowd. They were the sounds of someone singing. Someone was singing, unaccompanied at all. The song sounded familiar. I could recall its title, "Today I Confess My Love," the very song the choir sang together for the festival twenty years earlier. Who was singing was unclear. It didn't sound like me or like any of the old choir members. It wasn't Syncopation D's voice, either. The solo turned into a duet, then a trio, a quartet, a quintet, and so on. It became a chorus, an out-of-tune, off-the-beat chorus.

"Twenty-two tone-deaf people are singing the very same song from twenty years ago," said Syncopation D's voice through the wireless headset. "This is the mix that I've made of the voices of only my favorite tone-deaf people. Enjoy."

The lights were still out. The song was playing in pitch-darkness. Despite or maybe because of the dark, the song sounded beautiful. They were hitting different notes, but they didn't sound wrong. They sounded like they were singing in harmony. This may be the effect of singing in the dark. The song of the tone-deaf people sank in somewhere, like a left hand groping for the light switch in a dark room. Nobody laughed. A few even sang along with the chorus. The first verse was followed by piano sounds. Then the lights came on. Double Dubbing started playing the interlude of "Today I Confess My Love," drawing applause from the crowd. Some whistled. Others shouted bravo.

As the tone-deaf people began singing the second verse, Double Dubbing stopped playing, for the obvious reason that the musical instruments would only interfere with their singing. The song of the twenty-two people was in a subtle harmony. The secret may've been Syncopation D's remixing in the right places. Their voices were superimposed on one another, but never ruining one another, never ruining the song.

The old choir members in the front seats looked like they were remembering something that had become blurry and remote. They were all singing along, mouthing. I found myself singing along, too. It was an old song, but all of the lyrics came back to me. Unlike twenty years ago, it was us this time that were lip-synching. To the singing of the tone-deaf people, we moved our mouths, singing along but without making a sound. I just moved my mouth. The other old choir members seemed to be movingtheirs. We were thinking that that was how to show our respect for Syncopation D.

Born in 1971 in Kimcheon, a southeastern city of South Korea, KIM JUNGHYUK graduated from the Department of Korean Language and Literature at Keimyung University. He debuted as a writer in 2000 when his novella, "Penguin News," was published in the *Literature and Society* magazine.

KIM SO-YOUNG is a professional translator with over a decade of experience and a master's degree in translation and consecutive interpretation. She is currently focused on translating Korean books (fiction or nonfiction) into English.